the misadventures of
NOBBIN SWILL

Croaked!

LISA HARKRADER

**YELLOW
JACKET**

 **YELLOW JACKET**
an imprint of Little Bee Books
251 Park Avenue South, New York, NY 10010
Copyright © 2020 by Lisa Harkrader
All rights reserved, including the right of reproduction
in whole or in part in any form.
Yellow Jacket and associated colophon are trademarks
of Little Bee Books.
Manufactured in China RRD 0720
First Edition
10 9 8 7 6 5 4 3 2 1
Library of Congress Cataloging-in-Publication Data is available
upon request.

ISBN 978-1-4998-0973-2 (hc) / 978-1-4998-0974-9 (ebook)
yellowjacketreads.com

For more information about special discounts on bulk purchases,
please contact Little Bee Books at sales@littlebeebooks.com.

For Heather and Lee, my childhood partners in crime

Contents

Forest

Witch's
Cottage

Dwarfs'
Cottage

Woodcutter's
Cottage

Twigg

Butcher

Baker

Candlestick
Maker

Mill
Pond

Swill
Cottage

Dell

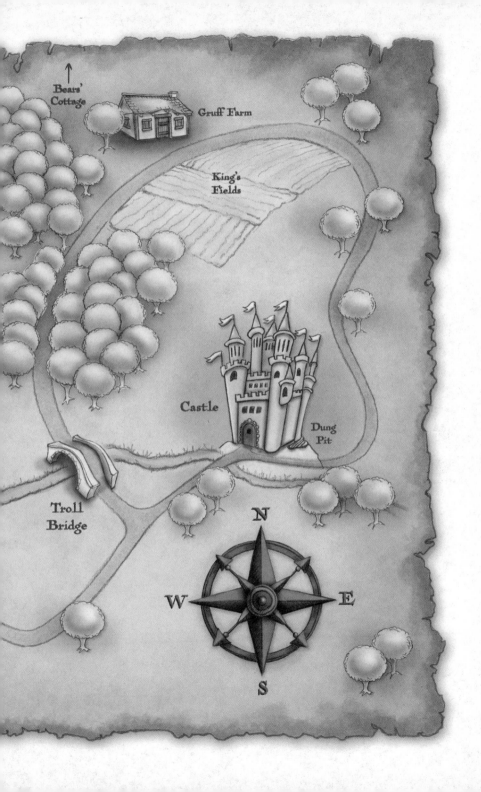

1

A Message in a Scroll

Once upon a time, I was Prince Charming's assistant. I never meant to be. I never hoped to be. For a time, I very much tried not to be.

But now I was, and was sorely glad of it.

"You there." Charming's father, the king, waved a finger toward me. "Nobbin."

I straightened. And swallowed. I might be the prince's assistant, but I was not well used to being summoned by the king. I inched a step closer to him.

We were on the castle balcony. The sun's first rays cast a soft glow over the castle's stone walls. The grass sparkled with dew in the courtyard. Thistlewick, the castle butler, kept a sharp eye on a pair of footmen who made their way through the crowd, serving tea.

We had gathered to watch Charming's prince training. Today's lesson: Gallantry, also known as The Rescuing of Damsels, Whether They Needed It or Not.

My feet fairly itched to be at Charming's side. I was doing him little good up on the balcony.

The king frowned. "Does the prince seem nervous?"

I peered across the courtyard. Folk from the village of Twigg were clustered around to watch. At the far end, Prince Charming held the reins of his steadfast steed, Darnell.

As I watched, the prince pulled the helmet from his head and held it against his breastplate. Not long ago, he'd lost the helmet's original plume in a bargain with the village peddler. He'd replumed it with a feather even taller and plumier than the last one. Now sunlight broke over the castle battlements, casting a beam over the prince. His plume glistened. His face glowed. His armor gleamed in a blinding sheen.

"No, sire," I said, well pleased I could give the king good news without having to lie.

"He looks calm," I said.

"Unruffled," I said.

The prince flung an armored hand toward the onlookers, startling poor Darnell.

"Confident he knows what he's doing," said I.

The king sighed. "That's what I was afraid of."

I did not mention that the prince had brought good fortune with him. I spied it in the cuffs of his armored gauntlets. One held a mitten. Someone had left it behind after a castle ball some weeks back. Charming did not know how to give it back, so he'd tucked it in his gauntlet for luck.

After the latest ball, the prince had found a woolen sock. Just the one. Now I spied it poking from his other gauntlet.

Charming took notice of us watching.

"Worry not, Father," he cried out. "Today is the day I make you proud." He pressed his palm to the breastplate of his armor. "I feel it."

"Yes," murmured the king. "I feel something, too." But he gave the prince an encouraging thumbs-up.

At the other end of the courtyard, the great tower soared to the sky. Sir Hugo scuttled back and forth at its base, paging through notes, checking items off a list, and tugging at the braided rope that dangled from the tower window to check that it was secure. At last, he unfurled a small flag emblazoned with the king's colors.

Ulff edged to the balcony rail next to me. He tipped his head toward Prince Charming.

"Me being his faithful guard and you being his noble assistant and all," Ulff muttered, "we should be down there, guarding and assisting. Leastways keeping him from falling off his horse."

I couldn't disagree.

"And we would be, too." Ulff's mutter dropped to a whisper. His bristly red face bristled and reddened. "If that scurvy Sir Roderick hadn't ordered us away."

I swiped a peek at Sir Roderick. And shivered. It was as if a dark, cold place followed Sir Roderick around and shot a chill through me every time I chanced a look at him.

He stood in his usual spot behind the king, one hand on the king's throne. He was the king's advisor. Also his cousin. Also third in line to the throne, behind Charming and his sister. Sir Roderick did not like coming in third.

I wrenched my gaze back to Ulff.

"But the prince himself thought it was a good idea," I said.

"You can't always go by him." Ulff shot a sideways glance at a steaming dish on a footman's tray. "The prince thought porridge was a good idea in place of gingerbread."

That was true enough. The prince had thought a hearty bowl of boiled oats would best fortify the crowd for a spirited demonstration of gallantry.

Ulff shook his head. "He's a fine prince. But we need to keep him away from the bears' cottage. He's lately summoned up too much enthusiasm for food that isn't frosted."

Before I could answer, a trumpet's blare pierced the balcony. Footmen flinched. Lords and ladies winced. The king closed his eyes. Sir Roderick ran a finger over his thin black mustache, pressing down a corner of his mouth that threatened to break into a smile.

A messenger, outfitted in the king's livery, strode across the balcony. He stopped before the king, tucked his trumpet under his arm, and, with a flourish, held out a parchment scroll. It was tightly rolled and secured with a wax seal of the deepest green.

I puzzled over this. The king received many
messages. Each was sealed with wax of the sender's
colors and pressed with an imprint of the sender's own
design. I hadn't before seen a wax that color. Or a
design such as this of a fat, round leaf.

The king narrowed his eyes at the scroll. He
flicked a glance at Sir Roderick, who was carefully
looking elsewhere.

Finally, the king took the scroll from the
messenger's hand. He studied it for a long moment,
then, without unsealing or unrolling it, clasped it

under his hand against the arm of his chair.

He waved his other hand at Sir Hugo. "Do let's get on with it."

Sir Roderick slid a glance toward the parchment. And smiled.

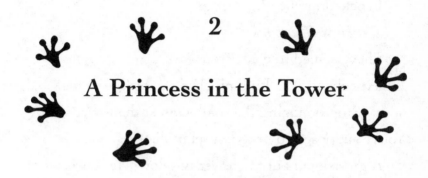

2
A Princess in the Tower

Sir Hugo gripped the flag. "Ready, Your Highness?" he called to the prince.

"Good sir, your tutelage does me honor." Charming bowed his head and flourished an armored hand toward Sir Hugo. "I bid you commence." The prince's way of saying, "Ready."

Sir Hugo raised the flag. A hush fell over the courtyard.

Except for:

Thu-bunk. Thu-bunk.

Thumps echoed over the castle grounds.

Thu-bunk. Thu-bunk.

I cocked my head.

Thu-bunk. Thu-bunk.

They seemed to come from—

"Angelica!" The king pinched the bridge of his nose. "Stop bouncing that ball against the tower wall. You're supposed to be a damsel in distress."

A girl leaned out the tower window. Her curls were tangled, her crown askew. She held a small leather ball in her hand, and she'd pushed up one sleeve of her puffy gown to get a better swing with her throwing arm.

She was Charming's younger sister, Her Royal Highness the Princess Angelica.

"I *am* distressed," she said. "You would be, too, if you had to wear this stupid princess outfit and sit in this stupid tower waiting for your brother to try some stupid rescue. I can climb down by myself, you know."

"Yes." The king clenched the scroll tightly. "We know."

"Poor child." Sir Roderick clucked his tongue. "She's never learned how a princess is meant to behave."

The king sighed. "Do try to cooperate, Angelica."

10

He flicked a hand at Sir Hugo. "Pray continue."

Sir Hugo clapped his hands. "Places, everyone."

Prince Charming gripped Darnell's reins. Angelica slumped back into the tower room. The crowd fell silent once more.

Sir Hugo raised his flag.

And according to the lesson plan, this is what was supposed to happen next:

1. At Sir Hugo's signal, the prince would leap onto Darnell's back.

2. Charming and Darnell would gallop to the tower, where the damsel in distress (in this case, Princess Angelica) was being held prisoner (or, in Angelica's case, complaining loudly about how bored she was and could she please go play rounders instead?—the dwarfs couldn't start the game without her).

3. Charming would neatly dismount and climb the damsel's hair up to the window. (In this case, rope braided to look like hair. This was a training exercise, after all. No need to involve real hair. Especially not hair growing from the head of Princess Angelica, who was in a foul mood already.)

11

4. Charming would climb back down, carrying
   Angelica, thus rescuing the damsel from her
   terrible fate, and also passing his
   Test of Gallantry.

This is what actually happened:

With a whip of his wrist, Sir Hugo lowered the
flag. Charming leapt for his saddle.

And in that moment, in that leap, the prince was
gallantry itself, all gleaming armor and plumy plume—

—until his gleaming armored foot hit one of
Darnell's stirrups.

His foot slipped. His plume flipped. He pitched
over backward, bounced once, and skidded under
Darnell's belly.

The king groaned. The crowd moaned. Ulff
clutched my arm as I clutched the balcony rail. Darnell
turned his head toward the prince and gave Charming
a sympathetic nicker.

"All is well," Charming called out.

He lay in the grass, rocking on his backplate,
much like a turtle flipped over on its shell. Sir Hugo
scrambled across the courtyard toward him.

Angelica propped her elbows on the windowsill,

her rounders ball clasped in one hand.

"I have a question," she said.

"Of course she does," Sir Roderick murmured.

"The prince is supposed to climb the damsel's hair," said Angelica. "I'm not sure how he'll do it without breaking her neck, but let's say he does. Won't they both be stuck?"

Sir Hugo had pulled Charming to his feet and was hoisting him onto Darnell—or trying to, leastways. The prince still teetered over the saddle on his belly.

Now Sir Hugo looked up, face creased in confusion. "I don't follow."

"The hair's supposed to be growing out of the damsel's head." Angelica tapped the ball against her head to demonstrate. "How can he carry her and still use her hair to climb down?"

"Heavens," murmured Sir Roderick, "the little dear has lost all control."

The king clenched the scroll so tight, his veins bulged into blue ropes on the back of his hand.

Sir Hugo pulled a leather-bound book from beneath his tunic. He flipped through the parchment pages. He flipped, flipped again, flipped once more, and sighed. He closed the book with a thud.

"There's nothing in the training manual." He chewed his lip. "Okay, here's what we do. Once the prince gets up to the tower, he'll cut off the princess's hair and tie it to something sturdy. Then he can climb back down with her."

Angelica nearly fell out the window. "Cut off her *hair*? That doesn't sound gallant."

The crowd didn't think so, either. They gasped and shot squinty looks at Sir Hugo.

"Folks." Sir Hugo held up his hands. "We're talking about rope here."

The crowd mumbled.

"It's not real hair," said Sir Hugo.

The crowd grumbled.

"The prince has to get down *somehow*."

The grumble grew to a growl.

The king closed his eyes. Sir Roderick stroked his mustache.

"The *prince*," said Angelica, "doesn't have to do *anything*. I don't need to be rescued."

She flung her arm for emphasis. The ball broke loose and soared over the courtyard—straight toward Prince Charming. It tore through the feathers of

Charming's plume and thumped Darnell square on the rump.

Darnell—startled—snorted and reared. He bolted from the courtyard, the prince jouncing sideways on his back.

The crowd stood in shocked silence. Ulff dug his fingers into my arm. I dug my fingers into the balcony rail. Sir Hugo dropped the manual and sprinted after horse and rider.

"Oh, dear," murmured Sir Roderick. "Something really must be done."

"Yes." The king squeezed the scroll near in half. "Angelica!"

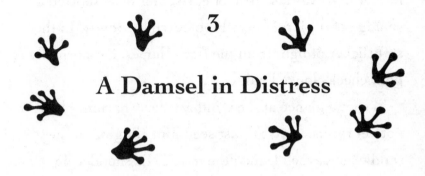

3

A Damsel in Distress

Ulff and I stood side by side in a corner of the king's library. We had spent the morning worrying what disaster Charming might make of his gallantry test.

We did not think to worry about his sister.

"The princess usually takes care of herself," Ulff whispered.

I nodded. "I think that's the problem."

I glanced at Angelica. She stood waiting before her father. Or rather, before the wide, heavy-legged table that served as her father's writing desk. And before the green-sealed scroll the king had placed in the center of it. Her hair was a scuffle of curls. Her nose sported a smudge of dirt from her climb down the tower. In the soft flicker of light from the fire's flames, her normally pink cheeks looked pale.

I shot a glance at the window. For Charming had not yet returned. We'd last seen him clinging to the saddle as Darnell leaped the moat. His shuddering voice trailed behind him: "All is well. I shall return . . . anonnn . . ."

Ulff caught me looking, for he'd been looking, too.

"The prince'll turn up," he whispered. He gave a crisp bob of his head, more to convince himself than me, I think. "And Darnell with him."

I nodded, more to convince me than him.

One of the housemaids stoked the fire until its embers roared to a blaze. She passed Anglica as she left the room, whisking the dirt from the princess's nose. A footman had retrieved Angelica's ball from the courtyard. As he set the silver tea tray on the king's table, he quitely slipped it to Angelica behind his back. Thistlewick moved past, carrying the candelabra, and straightened the small golden crown on Angelica's head.

When the king gave his hands a final rub, turned

from the fire, and settled his gaze on her, Angelica was nearly presentable.

He studied her, then shook his head. He waited until both housemaid and footman were gone and the heavy wooden door had clicked shut behind them. He cleared his throat.

"This is your home," he told Angelica. "I have always wanted you here, close to me."

"It's what I've always wanted, too," she said, her voice small, much too small for Angelica.

"Yes, well," said the king. "I see now I was being selfish. Certain things are expected of a royal princess. I don't know how to teach you those things, and you clearly haven't learned on your own. Sir Roderick believes—"

He flicked a glance at Sir Roderick, who lounged in a chair by the fireplace, carefully straightening the cuffs of his robe.

"—and I agree, that you need the guidance of someone who understands what a young princess requires. In short, you need the influence of a woman."

The influence of a woman. I spun this thought. As different as we were, in one way, maybe the most important way, Angelica and I—and Charming—were every bit alike. We had each of us grown up without a mother. Their mother, the queen, had died when Angelica was born, Charming but a toddling baby. What had become of my own mother, I had no inkling. My father wouldn't talk of it and would not tolerate my brothers talking of it, either.

So I could understand the king's point a small bit. I glanced at him. But what woman was he thinking of?

Angelica must have been spinning a similar thought.

"A woman?" She stared at her father, her face pinched in confusion. "But—I have *you*. That's all I need."

"No." The king shook his head. "I fear it's not. Not anymore."

He studied the scroll for some moments before unfurling it and spreading it on the table before him. He gave a nod to Thistlewick, who set the candelabra on the top edge of it, the better to cast light over the message, and the better to keep the scroll from scrolling back into itself.

The king pulled a pair of reading glasses from his robes and put them on. "Sir Roderick has found a royal family that may be of help. The queen is a distant relative of his. From a distant kingdom."

"Very distant," said Sir Roderick.

The king arched an eyebrow at Sir Roderick, then turned back to Angelica. "She has sent word. She's willing to take you on, er, in."

"In?" The word escaped Angelica's lips as scarcely more than a breath. "To . . . her castle?"

The king nodded.

I stared at Ulff. He stared at me. The bristles of his eyebrows bunched themselves into a troubled heap.

It wasn't right that Angelica had grown up without a mother.

But to send her away? To a distant kingdom? With strangers? I darted a glance at the king. Surely that was worse.

The king perched the glasses on his nose and peered down at the parchment. "She has agreed to take you under her wing. Share her skills and knowledge." He ran his finger down the list. "Surround you with the manners and customs of her royal court."

"Surround me?" Angelica's mouth dropped open.

"Begging your pardon, sire." Thistlewick coughed. "Might I offer a suggestion?"

21

"A *suggestion*?" Sir Roderick rolled his eyes to the ceiling. "Your *Majesty*—"

The king ignored him.

"Please do," he told Thistlewick. "I'm in sore need of suggestions at present."

Thistlewick took a breath.

"If it is a woman's influence you require," he said, "might I point out that our own castle is fairly brimming with women? Not women who are royal personages, certainly, but women who have *served* royal personages, women who have vast knowledge of the ways in which royal personages behave. Any one of them would be honored to offer her services. There is, for example, Mrs. Chumley."

Sir Roderick snorted. "The housekeeper?"

"The housekeeper!" Angelica blinked. "Yes! Mrs. Chumley could be my Sir Hugo. Charming has prince training. I can have princess training. Instead of gallantry and valor and hatcheting things up with a broadsword, I will learn, well, I'll learn to—to—"

Curtsy, I thought. I squeezed shut my eyes, thinking that if I thought the thought hard enough, Angelica might think it as well. *Curtsy*.

"—to curtsy!" she said.

I popped open my eyes. Hard thinking had worked! I tried to think what else I'd learned in the little time I'd spent at the castle.

"I shall learn to curtsy," said Angelica, "and—and—"

Wave, I thought. Hard. So hard, my forehead grew numb. *Wave like a princess*.

"—bow!" Angelica said at last. "I shall learn to bow." She frowned. "No, that's not right. Men bow. Women curtsy. I'll—I'll—"

Sir Roderick let out a dramatic sigh. "Poor child knows so little, she doesn't know how little she knows."

"No. I do," said Angelica. "I'll get this. There are things I should learn, and I'll learn them. Maybe this queen could send Mrs. Chumley a list. Or, no—a training manual! Like Sir Hugo has for Charming. And then—"

"*Sire*," said Sir Roderick. "You cannot think to trust our dear, *precious* Angelica—her character, her well-being, her very future to a"—his nostrils flared—"housekeeper."

The king mulled this for some moments.

"No," he said at last. "Perhaps not." He turned to Angelica. "Sir Roderick is right."

Ulff leaned toward me. "That weaselly knave's never been right in his egg-rotted life."

"If you're to learn these things," said the king, "you must learn them properly from the queen. And she can best teach them in her own castle."

Angelica stared up at him. "So . . . you're to just send me away?"

The king heaved a heavy sigh. "It's what's best, Angelica."

She swallowed.

Thistlewick bowed his head.

Ulff sniffed and wiped a sleeve across his nose.

Sir Roderick could no longer tamp down the corner of his mouth, and now it curled into an outright smirk.

I opened my mouth, but a great dry lump of helplessness lodged itself in my throat, choking off any words I might have thought to say.

Still. I balled my fists. Someone had to say something. Anything.

"Father!" A voice rang out from the hall.

The heavy door groaned open, and Prince

Charming clanked in. Sir Hugo scrambled behind, rubbing mud from the prince's elbow. Charming's new plume was flattened, his armor askew. Tufts of grass jutted from the hinges of his knee guards, and the lucky mitten dangled by one snagged thread from his gauntlet.

I took a step toward him, for I was his noble assistant. But Ulff poked a sharp elbow into my ribs and tipped his head. I followed his gaze.

From the prince's hand dangled the broken end of a rein, snapped loose from a horse's bridle.

Angelica spied it, too. She stared up at her brother. "Darnell?" Her voice quivered.

"Fit as a foal," said Charming, his own voice out of breath and not fit-sounding at all. "Groom is leading him to the stable for a brisk rubdown and well-deserved bucket of oats."

Ulff nodded. Angelica's shoulders sagged in relief. I let out a breath I hadn't known I'd been holding.

Charming came to stand behind his sister. His hair stood at odd angles and his cheeks were flushed pink, but he lifted his chin and leveled a gaze at his father.

"You cannot think to send Angelica away," he said. "She may not be a proper princess. At least, not

25

the sort one reads about in fairy tales. Or the sort troubadours tell about in song. Or the sort anyone has ever heard of, really."

Angelica looked up at him with a sharp frown.

"But she has the heart of a princess," he continued. "She is brave. She is kind. She is true. She is the best fielder the village rounders team has ever had." He placed an armored hand on Angelica's shoulder. "More than that," he said, "she is your daughter."

The king sat back, taking in the prince's words. He swiped a finger at the corner of his eye. He lowered his gaze to the parchment. His resolve seemed to waver.

But before he could speak, the liveried messenger strode into the library. He carried another scroll. This one, too, was tightly rolled, sealed with wax of green.

"Plague and pestilence." The king let out a sharp breath. "What is it now?"

The messenger snapped his heels together and lifted his trumpet to his lips.

"Truly." The king held up a hand. "That isn't necessary."

The messenger looked at the king. He looked at his trumpet. His shoulders drooped, and his chin quivered.

The king sighed. "Very well." He waved a hand. "Proceed."

The messenger's shoulders perked up. He placed the trumpet to his lips and let out a rousing blast.

DOOT-da-DOOOOOOO!

Charming flinched. Sir Roderick winced. Ulff and Angelica pressed fingers to their ears, and the king held a hand over his closed eyes until the last of the blare had echoed away. Only Thistlewick seemed to withstand it with but the merest clench of his shoulders to give him away.

The messenger gave a satisfied nod, tucked the trumpet under his arm, and unsealed the scroll.

As he unfurled it, a chill swept through the room, billowing the draperies and setting the flames of the candelabra aflicker.

I caught my breath. Beside me, Ulff shivered and rubbed his hands over his arms.

The messenger held the message before him. "Her Royal Majesty Queen Ermintrude and her son, His Royal Highness Prince Figbert," he announced, "have arrived."

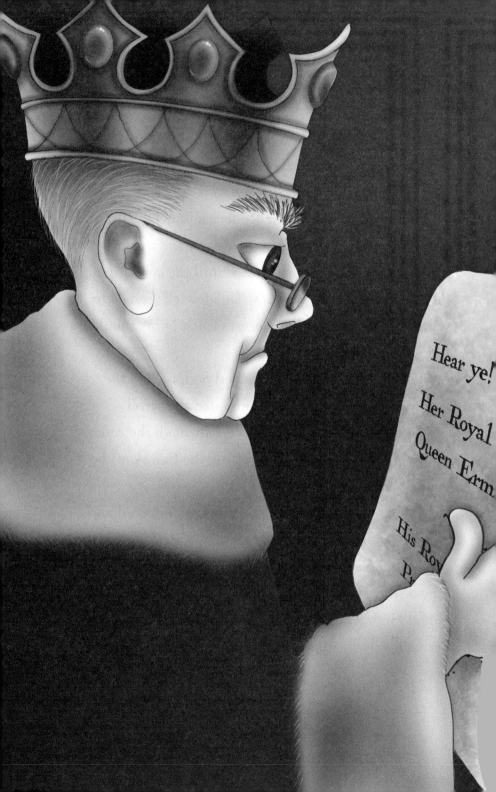

Hear ye!

Her Royal

Queen Erm

His Roy

P

4

A Carriage in the Courtyard

Ghe's arrived?" The king's voice thundered.

He rose, his great chair letting out a great groan.
He plucked this latest scroll from the messenger's
livery-gloved hands. He scanned his eyes over its
lettering.

"I had no warning she would be here so soon." The
king shot a look at Sir Roderick. "I only just received
word this morning she was coming at all."

"Ah. Well." Sir Roderick waved a hand in the air
with a flourish. "You can see how impressive she is
already. Punctuality *is* a virtue."

Charming frowned. "And she's brought her son?"

"It seems so." The king flicked a hand against the parchment. "She made no mention of him before."

Sir Roderick waved this off as well. "Meant as a surprise, no doubt. A chance to observe her skillful training of a young royal."

"Yes. Well. She's here now." The king cast the parchment on his desk. "Thistlewick?"

Thistlewick lifted his chin. "On top of the matter, sire."

He gave a brisk bow, turned on his heels, and strode from the room. The messenger scuttled out in his wake. Sir Hugo tugged a tuft of grass from Charming's armor, then followed.

The king crossed to the window, his thick fur robes trailing across the carpets.

Angelica scrambled up onto the window seat in front of him. Charming moved to his father's side. Ulff and I slipped in next to the prince. Roderick hovered at the rear, the firelight casting a dark shadow of him over window and wall.

We kept ourselves well hidden behind the draperies and peered down at the courtyard below.

A carriage, black and gleaming, had stopped on the

cobbled drive. Its trim was the same green as the wax on the parchment scrolls, and emblazoned on the top was the same fat leaf that was imprinted in the seal.

One of the king's footmen stepped forward and opened the carriage door. He bowed low and extended a gloved hand.

Another hand clasped his, and a woman emerged from the carriage. She was small, but seemed to fill more than her share of space, all wide skirts and swinging robes. A glittering crown sat atop her head.

She stepped to the cobblestones and stood for a moment, head tipped, gloved finger to her chin, studying the castle. She took in the whole of it, much like Mr. Stiltskin, the village peddler, sizing up a bauble he wished to bargain for. Her gaze swept to the upper reaches of the castle, and all of us, even the king, wrenched our heads back from the window.

After a moment, we craned forward for another peek.

From the carriage stepped a young boy.

Ulff leaned in, placing a bristled red hand against the window glass. "Is that the prince?"

"It would seem so," said the king.

I leaned in for a better look, too. When the messenger had announced that a Prince Figbert had arrived, I expected a prince much like our Charming: tall and shiny in steel-plated armor. But this prince was younger. More my age. Or Angelica's. In place of armor, he wore a swirl of velvet and fur, like his mother.

Prince Figbert pushed past the footman and marched into the castle. His mother swept in behind him.

"They have indeed arrived." The king sighed. "I

suppose we should give them time to settle in. We shall have a dinner reception this evening to greet them. I'll let Thistlewick know."

He turned to leave. Angelica scrambled down from the window seat after him. Charming trailed behind, and Ulff followed. I started to leave, too, but thought to steal one last glimpse.

As I peered down, another passenger teetered down from the carriage, weighted down by a mountain of swaying bags and cases. A lady's maid, by the look of her stern black dress.

The footman scrambled to tuck a fallen umbrella back into her stack of luggage and lift a trunk for her. Then he poked his head into the carriage door. After giving the inside a thorough look, he stepped back and swung it shut. He gave a rap on the side of the carriage, and it trundled away.

I frowned. The queen had brought only one maid. Odd.

I turned to leave—

—and ran headlong into Sir Roderick. Or leastways, into Sir Roderick's robed belly.

"Oh!" I took a step back.

Sir Roderick stared down at me, one eyebrow

raised. "Careful, young Nobbin." His mustache twitched into a sneer. "Heed where you're going, or you may run into something you wished to avoid."

5

A List of Crimes

Ulff was waiting in the hall.

"Our prince'll want to look presentable to meet the queen," he said. "He'll be shining his armor."

I nodded. We both knew where he'd be shining it.

We wound our way through passages, down stairways, and out the small side door by the kitchens. We started across the courtyard, our feet crunching over gravel and stone.

We'd been quiet on our journey. But now that we were outside the listening ears of the castle, Ulff put a hand on my arm. He slowed his walk to cast a quick glance about the courtyard.

"It's a peculiar day, Nobbin." He leaned his head close to mine. "Started out same as always, the prince charging off on his princely business, us wondering what sticky sort of wicket he'd get himself into and how we'd get him out. But here it is not even yet noonday yet, and already the king's announced he's sending Princess Angelica away, and before you can get your eyes good and blinked, a queen's here to fetch her." He shook his head. "I can't hardly wrap my mind around it."

I swallowed. I couldn't wrap my mind around it, either. The princess could be prickly. Prickly as a blackberry bramble. But also like a blackberry bramble, tough and lively and sometimes quite sweet. A small, sweet, prickly bramble whirling through the castle.

I tried to think what the castle would be like with her gone.

Ulff seemed to read my thoughts. "It'll be a darker place, for sure."

I nodded. "I keep thinking there has to be something we can do."

"Well." Ulff chewed his lip, the bristles of his cheek poking this way and that. "When the prince takes us galavanting out to investigate, you make lists. Clues. Suspects. Whatever whatnot we need to solve the puzzle. Might do us good to make a list now."

I shot him a look, surprised I hadn't thought of this very thing. I rummaged in my tunic and rustled out a scrap of paper, along with a broken stub of a pencil.

I slowed enough to write How to Maybe Save Angelica at the top of the page.

Ulff gave a nod. "First," he said, "what about we hobble the queen's carriage?"

I looked up. "Hobble? You mean . . . wreck?"

"Not wreck. More like, refashion. We could take off a wheel. And misplace it. In the moat maybe. That'd stop Angelica leaving, for sure."

"Only until the village wheelwright came to put on a new one." Now I was the one chewing my lip. "But it could buy us some time."

I wrote it on the list.

"Here's an idea," I said. "We could sprinkle Angelica with pepper. Every time the queen got near her, she'd sneeze." I started scribbling it down.

"Sneeze?" Ulff knotted his brows. Then his eyes grew wide. "Like an allergy! The queen wouldn't take the princess to her castle if she thought she was allergic to her. You're a smart lad, Nobbin."

He punched my arm in admiration.

"Oh!" he said. "I know! We could give the king a potion to change his mind."

I rubbed the sore spot on my arm and started to write POTION.

I stopped and looked up. "You can make potions?"

"Well, no," he said. "That's a stumbling block. But

40

write it down. If it turns out we do need a potion, I could likely learn."

I shrugged. We didn't have anything better at this point. I put it on the list.

Ulff and I traded ideas all the way across the courtyard.

As we neared the stable, I studied the scrap of paper.

How to
Maybe Save Angelica

1. Hobble the queen's carriage
2. Sprinkle Angelica with pepper
3. Give the king a potion
4. Disguise Angelica as a chambermaid
5. Kidnap the queen
6. Kidnap Angelica
7. Kidnap Prince Figbert and not give him back until the king changes his mind (or until we can't bear having Figbert around anymore, whichever comes first)

I frowned. Normally, my lists helped us solve crimes. But this was more a list of crimes we were thinking to commit. I wondered if we were veering down the wrong path.

We'd just reached the stable door when I heard: "Give Angelica secret princess lessons so she can act a proper princess in front of the queen and convince her father not to send her away."

"Excellent!" I began writing it down.

My pencil scritched to a halt.

It *was* an excellent idea.

But it had not come from Ulff.

I looked up.

Angelica stood before the stable door, arms crossed, chin thrust out.

6

A Princess in Training

We found Charming perched on a bundle of straw beside Darnell's stall. He was, in turns, rubbing the gleam back into his breastplate with all the force his muscles could muster, and scratching Darnell on the forelock.

At the sound of our feet scuffing over the stone floor, prince and horse looked up.

"Knobs on a neckerchief!" Charming cried at the sight of us. "Are we summoned to the dinner reception already?"

"Not yet," said Ulff. "You've still got time to make yourself nice and shiny."

"And?" Angelica looked from me to Ulff and back again.

"And," I said, "time to make the princess nice and, well, princess-like."

"Princess-like?" Charming glanced at his sister. At her gown, torn at the hem and grass-stained at the knee, one sleeve still pushed up for better throwing. "By dinner?"

She glowered at him. "I can change my clothes," she said. "I just need to know how to walk properly. And eat properly. And speak only when spoken to."

"Whoo. That'll be the tough one," said Ulff.

She gave him a scowl, then turned to her brother. "I need to know enough princess stuff so Father will notice and be well pleased. So he won't send me off with that—that"—she flipped a hand toward the castle—"Ermintrude." She sighed. Her shoulders drooped. "What I need," she said, "is princess training."

Charming, a staunch champion of his own training with Sir Hugo, nodded.

He narrowed his eyes. He tipped his head. He looked his sister up and down.

"Nobbin," he said, "make a list."

We made the list. And it was a good one.

Things Angelica Must Know Before Dinner

1. the royal curtsy
2. the royal wave
3. how to hold a teacup
4. how to sit like a princess with ankles politely crossed to the side
5. which fork to use for salad
6. which fork to use for fish
7. how not use any fork at any time to poke annoying dinner guests or move the tart tray closer to one's plate
8. to always use an indoor voice and never exclaim "swine buckets!" no matter how annoying those dinner guests may be
9. to politely and discreetly use a napkin to wipe one's hands or face

We spent the afternoon going through drills.

We practiced how to curtsy.

And wave.

And hold a teacup daintily in two fingers.

Angelica did splosh a bit of tea on her gown. And she had a worrying habit of propping her elbow on the table, head in her hand. But she only cursed once, and by the time we had to rush back to the castle to change for dinner, she had stopped wiping her nose on her sleeve entirely.

As we turned to leave the stable, she stopped.

She stood looking up at us, eyes wide, fingers crossed. "Do you think I'm ready?"

Ulff and Charming and Darnell and I looked at each other. We looked at Angelica.

Charming straightened the crown upon her head. He nodded.

"Yes," he said. "You're ready."

7

A Wobble in the Curtsy

She's not ready!" hissed Ulff.

I darted a glance, looking for sign of the princess.

We were gathered in the drawing room, awaiting the arrival of the queen and her son. The maids had polished the place till light glinted from every surface—the crystal of the chandeliers, the marble of the fireplace, even the gold braid of the footmen's livery.

Lords and ladies stood clustered in groups. Footmen wove among them holding gleaming silver trays. Glasses tinkled. Voices murmured. Now and again someone let out a small laugh. Thistlewick stood at his post by the door, announcing each guest as they arrived.

My glance fell on the king. He held court in the center of the room, Charming at his side. On his other side, as always, stood Sir Roderick.

Ulff and I had stashed ourselves beside a nearby suit of armor, but Roderick must have sensed me watching. He glanced across the room, picked me out from the armor, and fired a glare at me so black and cold, it shot a chill through my very bones.

I shuddered and pulled my gaze away.

And finally spied Angelica.

During any other castle party, she would be sprawled on one of the couches, hands filled with cards, whichever footman she'd talked into playing piquet with her standing straight and tidy at her side.

But now she waited quietly beside her father, or rather, in the shadow of her father. She had tucked herself between the king and Prince Charming and stood clutching and unclutching the skirt of her gown.

"She's ready enough," I said. "Readier than she was this morning. If she remembers to keep her gloves on to stop her licking her fingers and doesn't take up rounders practice with the serving spoons and buns, the king should well be pleased."

"Pleased," said Ulff. "Or flabbergasted."

As he reached for a slice of gingerbread from a passing footman's tray, a hush fell over the room. I looked up. Lords and ladies turned toward the door.

Thistlewick, still stationed there, lifted his chin.

"Presenting Her Royal Majesty Queen Ermintrude," he announced, "and His Royal Highness Prince Figbert."

The queen swept into the room in a swirl of green and gold. Lords and ladies parted to make room for her—and for her skirts. For her skirts were massive, wider than three of the queen put together. They bobbed along, seemingly on their own, like a separate creature altogether.

"She could fit three goats and a pony under there," Ulff grunted, "and no one would be the wiser."

A boy, shorter than me, strolled in at her side. His head was rather small, his mouth wide, and he had very little chin to speak of. But he was resplendent in green and gold, like his mother. He glanced about the drawing room, looking each vase and candlestick up and down, as if judging whether it were worthy of his notice.

The queen's maid trailed behind the both of them. She was younger than I'd first thought. Barely more than a girl. It was the stiff bleakness of her dress that had made her seem older from afar. She fluttered after her mistress, fluffing the queen's robes and straightening the queen's skirts.

I studied those skirts. For all their splendid elegance, I couldn't help noticing a careful mend along the hem. The maid caught me looking, gave the skirt a firm shake, and the mend disappeared.

I blinked and shook my head. Perhaps I hadn't seen it at all.

The queen glided to a stop before the king. A swirl of perfume billowed about her, cloaking the room in its sweet, flowery scent.

Ulff sneezed.

The king covered a sudden cough.

"Your Majesty." Queen Ermintrude dropped low in a full, regal curtsy.

Angelica, partly hidden by her father's great robes, studied her, half copying the queen's movements with her own hands and feet.

The king dipped his head. "An honor to meet you." He turned. "And you must be Prince Figbert. How do you do?"

"Fine," said Figbert, looking rather bored until his mother flicked a finger against the back of his neck.

Figbert straightened.

"I mean, very well, Your Majesty. Thank you." He bent low in a surprisingly impressive bow.

"I must apologize." The queen settled a hand on Prince Figbert's shoulder. "Darling Figgy was so delighted to be here, for a moment he was rendered utterly speechless."

Ulff looked at me. *Figgy?* he mouthed.

I shrugged.

The king introduced Charming, with more bowing and curtsying all around.

"And I believe you know Sir Roderick," said the king.

Again, more bows and curtsies.

"And this"—the king fairly pulled Angelica from behind his robes—"is Princess Angelica."

Angelica chanced a look at Charming, who gave her an encouraging nod.

She took a breath and plunged into a curtsy, giving it an extra sweep and a swan-like flourish of her hands.

She wobbled a bit at the bottom and looked for a moment as if she might topple over. And she may well have if a passing footman hadn't sneaked a quick hand out to steady her.

The princess righted herself and rose. She even managed to say, "I'm so very pleased to make your acquaintance," in a voice quite pleasant and very little like Angelica's own.

The king raised his eyebrows for a surprised moment, then lifted his chest and placed a hand on Angelica's shoulder. He turned toward the queen and fairly beamed.

Sir Roderick also raised an eyebrow. But his look was dark as he threw a glare on the princess.

Figbert looked Angelica up and down. He puckered his face into a sneer.

"You must be the disaster of a princess," he said.

8

A Crowd in the Village

I am loath to say it," said Charming, "but the queen's quite impressive."

The king raised his eyebrows. "She's hard to miss. I'll give her that."

Sunlight shone in through the windows above us, casting the main hall of the castle in a pink morning glow. We waited—the king, Prince Charming, Sir Roderick, Angelica, Ulff, and I—for the queen and Prince Figbert to join us.

Last night, the first of the queen's visit, had been a success, more or less.

Angelica had knocked her crown askew once. She'd stumbled twice. And one time she nearly started talking with her mouth full—until Thistlewick passed by and lifted her chin with one finger to press shut her lips.

But she did remember to keep her ankles crossed and to respond politely when spoken to. And through it all, through every sneer and insult Figbert hurled, she had kept her thoughts—and her hands—to herself.

I'm certain it very near killed her.

"Our young princess did well," said Ulff.

I nodded. "I hope she can keep it up."

At last, Queen Ermintrude swept down the staircase, bobbing and shimmering in a completely different gown from last evening, a cloud of perfume bobbing with her.

I squinted. The gown did look different, but when I studied it closer, I saw that the queen—or her maid, more like—had simply switched up the layers of skirts from yesterday. Where at last night's reception she'd worn the green velvet layered over the gold, this morning the gold satin lay over the green. It was a clever trick. The queen looked for all the world as if she wore something new.

Figbert followed his mother down the stairs, his nose in the air. The maid—whose name, it turned out, was Lucy—scuttled behind.

The queen breezed to a stop before the king. "Your castle is simply adorable," she told him. "So very few rooms and only a handful of halls. Much easier to navigate than my enormous, sprawling castle. Although, truly, *castle* isn't the word for it. It's more of a palace, really."

Thunk.

With a vigorous heave, a pair of footmen lifted the heavy iron latches of the castle's main doors. They swung the doors wide, and the bunch of us paraded out into the warm sunshine of the courtyard.

The queen wrinkled her nose, and her maid scurried over to shade her mistress's face from the light.

"Where is it we're going?" the queen asked the king.

"Twigg," he replied.

"Twig?" She cocked her head. "Like a stick? Whyever would we want to see a stick?"

"Twigg," said the king, "like the village. Our local villagers were delighted to hear that a distant queen was visiting our small hamlet. A ride through Twigg will allow them to welcome you for themselves. And, er, Prince Figbert, too, of course."

Figbert's wide mouth stretched even wider. It may have been an attempt at a smile. But it looked more like he needed to belch.

"Ah, yes. Commoners." The queen sighed. "I don't imagine very many exciting things happen here to relieve the endless dreariness of their dark and dismal lives. The least I can do is provide one small spark of joy for them while I'm here. It may be the only joy they ever get."

The footmen stepped forward to open the doors of the carriages. For we had two of them. The queen and her skirts nearly filled the king's gilded coach, leaving only a sliver of space for the king, Sir Roderick, and the queen's maid. Angelica, then Figbert, then Ulff and

I climbed into the second smaller carriage.

Out in the courtyard, the groom and Sir Hugo boosted Charming onto Darnell's saddle.

We set out. Charming and Darnell took the lead, flanked by a number of the King's Men. Our small carriage creaked along after, with the king's coach after that. More King's Men brought up the rear, and a pair of pages marched ahead, brandishing the king's banner.

Angelica sat beside me, as far from Prince Figbert as one small carriage would allow. Ulff and Figbert swayed along on the other side.

Figbert squirmed in his seat, shifting this way and that, like a dog trying to find the right spot to lie down.

"I hardly slept last night," he sniffed. "Your castle is horridly uncomfortable."

Beside me, Angelica clenched her teeth.

"My bed was lumpy, my room cold," said Figbert. "The draperies were too thin to keep out the chill. We have much nicer draperies at home."

"Maybe you should go back there," Ulff muttered.

"Our garden pond is nicer, too," Figbert continued. "And our horses. I hardly believe Prince Charming lets anyone see him riding his hack of a horse. My mother has promised to get me a *real* steed as soon as we get home."

"Darnell," Angelica growled through gritted teeth, "is the finest horse *you'll* ever meet."

She clasped her skirt in balled fists, looking every inch as if she would lunge across the carriage at Figbert. I touched her arm, and she closed her eyes, blew out a breath, and smoothed the wrinkles of her gown.

The first house we came to, teetering at the very edge of Twigg, was mine.

Or at least, it used to be mine.

It was Swill Cottage, home to the Swills, dung farmers to the king. My brothers lived there, along with our father. And, till but recently, me.

We rolled past, with no one save me giving our rickety hovel a glance. My father and brothers did their work at night and slept this time of morning. The rumble of their four clashing snores followed us as we trundled on to the village proper.

All of Twigg, it seemed, had turned out to greet the queen.

They crowded along both sides of the high street,

waving small flags of the queen's royal green. The shops were aflutter with streamers, and the tailor had hoisted a large banner over the tailor shop window:

We rolled to a stop. The crowd let out a cheer.

Our carriage door squeaked open, and Angelica started to climb down, then rememberd to allow a footman to help her. Figbert stepped out, pushing the footman away entirely. Ulff and I scrambled out afterward. I was glad to be free of both carriage and Figgy.

Another footman stood beside the open door of the

king's coach, his gloved hand at the ready. A hush fell over the crowd.

Queen Ermintrude poked her head from the carriage. She saw the throng of villagers, lined up with their flags.

"Huzzah!" cried the crowd.

"Oh." The queen's face crinkled in distaste. "We're going to *meet* them."

A footman helped her from the carriage, then the king and Sir Roderick.

Lucy, the maid, scrambled after them, tripping as she reached the street and tumbling into the village peddler. The peddler set her upright, with more politeness than I ever imagined of him, and chatted with her for a moment. Then he tipped his hat and ambled off down the lane, the pots and cups inside his great coat rattling.

The king and Charming, with Angelica in tow, led Ermintrude and Figgy through the village. Ulff and I and the maid and Sir Roderick trailed behind.

And in the very short time we meandered through Twigg, Figbert managed to offend nearly everyone in town.

At the end of the lane, we stopped at the butcher's.

The queen was not interested in the cutting of meats.
Nor were any of us, but we tried to be polite. Except
Figbert, who refused to go into the shop at all. Which
deflated the poor butcher, who took great pride in his
skill.

As we neared the bake shop, the baker woman
ushered us in and proudly showed the queen her
gleaming bakery case filled with cakes. Figbert
ran a finger along the top of the case. He held it up.
"Grease," he said, and insisted the queen's maid wipe it
from his hand.

At the candlestick shop, Figbert flicked his finger against the candlestick maker's finest candlestick to see if the silver were real. When it let out the high, sweet *ping* of true silver, Figbert pinched his lips near to his nose and said, "Sounds like tin."

Queen Ermintrude took little notice of Figbert's rude manners. But she kept a sharp eye on Angelica.

As she waited for us all to leave the candlestick shop, Angelica nibbled her thumbnail.

Queen Ermintrude pointed this out to the king.

"A chewed nail isn't such a crime," said the king.

"It's not proper princess behavior," said Sir Roderick.

"I could cure her of it in an instant," said the queen.

As we headed back toward the carriage, a fly darted about Angelica's face. She batted it away, then scratched the spot on her nose where it had touched down.

Queen Ermintrude gasped.

"A princess never scratches," she said. "Ever."

"What if she has an itch?" said Ulff.

"I could take care of it in a trice," the queen told the king. "As well as her giggling and gum-chewing and fondness for forest folk—"

"But the dwarfs are fine young men," said Charming, "and jolly teammates."

"—and her off-key singing," said the queen, "and the way her hair curls all over her head in a most un-princess-like fashion."

The king studied Angelica, who was, in fact, chatting with the dwarfs—and giggling.

"I've never taken notice of any of that." He shook his head. "I truly have let her down."

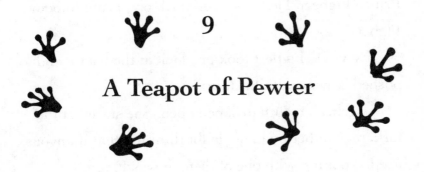

A Teapot of Pewter

"It's *us* who'll be letting our princess down," Ulff muttered. He unfolded his napkin, gave it a shake, and tucked it in his shirt collar. "If we can't find a way to keep her here."

A footman arrived with the tea. He served the king, then the queen.

Steam swirled from their cups and across the vast dining table, its surface spilling over with vases, flowers, and candles.

It was the last night of the queen's visit—Angelica's last chance to convince her father not to send her away with the queen.

The footman served Charming, then stepped beside Prince Figbert. He leaned forward, preparing to pour Figbert's tea.

"Ewww!" Figbert took one look at the teapot and pushed it away with his fork.

Angelica's mouth dropped open. She stared at the fork, then at her own, no doubt thinking that if anyone needed poking with one of them, it was Figgy.

"Does the castle always serve tea"—Figbert scowled at the teapot as if it had just crawled from the dung pit—"in *that*?"

The footman stepped back and held the pot protectively to his chest.

The queen patted Figbert's hand. "Figgy, dear," she said. "Remember we're guests here. We shouldn't point fingers at our hosts' tableware, no matter how wretched."

Roderick leaned toward the king. "You see how skilled she is at correcting young Figbert's manners?"

Queen Ermintrude gave the king an apologetic smile. "Poor Figgy. He's used to a much more, well, *elegant* tea service."

"Yes." The king raised an eyebrow at Thistlewick. "Aren't we all?"

Thistlewick stepped forward. "Apologies, Your Majesty," he told the queen, "but the good silver tea service seems to have been, ah, misplaced. It is most certainly in the kitchens . . . somewhere. In its absence, I have done my best to polish the pewter set. It has a few dents and dings, but it's finely crafted. It has served the royal family for hundreds of years. We will use the silver in the future, I assure you. Once it has been, ah, located."

"Missing silver?" The king let out a sigh. "Not this again."

"We had a rash of thefts here recently," Charming explained. He frowned. "But I thought my men and I had cleared that up."

The queen nodded knowingly. "That kind of thing rarely clears up when servants are of"—she lowered her voice to a whisper—"low character."

I stared. Ulff glared. Charming held out an arm to keep Thistlewick from storming the table.

"Low character?" The words flew from Angelica's lips before she could stop them. She gasped and clapped both hands over her mouth.

The king gripped the arms of his chair. "Our servants are of the highest character, I assure you." He kept his voice even. "None of them would entertain the slightest thought of taking something that did not belong to them."

"I suppose." The queen flipped a hand in the air. "You would know your servants better than I."

The king was spared from answering when another footman arrived with the soup, still bubbling in its tureen. I leaned forward for a whiff of its savory scent, for I knew exactly which soup Cook had whipped up for this dinner. And my watering mouth couldn't be more pleased.

Angelica reached for her spoon. Unfortunately, it was her teaspoon. Fortunately, Thistlewick had recovered himself. He quietly placed his thumb on the teaspoon to keep her lifting it from the table and slid her soup spoon into her hand.

Angelica gave him a grateful smile.

"Igh!"

We all looked across the table.

Figbert had sipped up a spoonful of soup, twisted his face into a grimace, and looked as if he were about to spit it back into his bowl. His mother placed her hand on his to stop him, and he managed to work the soup around in his mouth and swallow.

He stared at his bowl in horror. "What *is* that?"

"That," said Charming, "is Cook's well-loved pumpkin soup, the delight of all who have tasted it. She made it specially for tonight, thinking you might find it tasty."

"I don't." Figbert pushed his soup bowl away. "I thought you'd served up the dishwater by mistake."

Angelica had been watching him, hands gripping the table until her fingers had gone white. Her eyes narrowed. Her nostrils flared. Her jaw clenched till I thought her teeth might very well crack.

Ulff clutched my arm. I clutched my napkin—

—and caught Queen Ermintrude smiling at Prince Figbert . . . in satisfaction, it seemed. I pondered this. I'd first thought the queen took no notice of the rude things Figbert did. Now I wondered if she hoped he'd do more.

I glanced at Angelica, throwing daggers at the prince with her eyes.

For the ruder Figbert acted, the angrier Angelica became. And the angrier Angelica became, the more likely she would do something to displease her father.

Exactly what the queen—and Sir Roderick—wanted.

Angelica caught Sir Roderick watching her across

the table, a smug smile on his face. She took a breath, fixed her eyes on her soup bowl, and folded her hands—stiffly—in her lap.

Over the next four courses of dinner, Prince Figbert grumbled. He mumbled. He turned his nose up at the fish.

"Can't blame him there," Ulff whispered to me. "It does taste a mite fishy."

And then it was time for dessert.

"Finally!" Ulff rubbed his hands together.

He nearly passed out from joy when he glimpsed the dessert tray.

"Gingerbread!" he said.

It was indeed gingerbread. Fine gingerbread. For deep in the king's forest, on the far side of Twigg, there sat a cottage made entirely of gingerbread. The witch who lived there baked the gingerbread for it herself.

She had baked this gingerbread, too, special for the queen's arrival, a gift to welcome her.

My stomach was so full already, I scarce had room for one bite more. But as the footman circled the table and set a plate of the spicy brown gingerbread before me, my mouth watered.

I picked up my dessert fork, thinking to cut off a

goodly bite, when from across the table, Figbert let out another, *"Eeew."*

I looked up. He was staring at his gingerbread as if it were a dead thing he'd found in the roadway.

"I can't eat this," he said.

"Sure you can." Ulff forked up a chunk of his own gingerbread. "It's delicious. The witch uses only the finest flours and purest spices. I've seen them." He thrust the bite in his mouth, gave it a chew, and sighed.

Queen Ermintrude smiled down at him. "I'm sure you think so, dear," she said. "You've likely not ventured into the wider world."

Ulff swallowed and frowned.

"I've ventured," he muttered. "I've ventured plenty."

I started to reassure him that our hair-raising treks to the forest with Charming to investigate odd goings-on did count as venturing, when a strangled cry rang out from across the table.

"Blech!" Figbert wiped at his tongue. *"Pftht, pftht, pfthf, pftht, pftht."* He spit gingerbread into his napkin. "How can anyone eat this? It's like chewing a mouthful of mud."

The room when silent. Servants and dinner guests froze.

All but Angelica.

"That's *it*!" She snatched up her dessert fork, stabbed a large chunk of gingerbread, and held it before her. "You've insulted the teapot and been rude to the cook, and your mother called our servants low. Now you've besmirched the witch and her gingerbread. I'm finished being polite."

Figbert opened his mouth to protest.

Angelica pulled the tip of her fork back with her other hand and—*thwoop!*—let the gingerbread fly.

It flew across the table, shearing a leaf from a royal centerpiece and flickering the flame of a royal candle.

Figbert's mouth was still wide as he worked it into a whine. "*Ullp.*" The gingerbread shot inside. *Gulp.* He swallowed it whole.

Angelica stabbed another chunk of gingerbread, but the king grasped her wrist before she could let it fly.

He looked at Sir Roderick.

"Let's see about this agreement," he said.

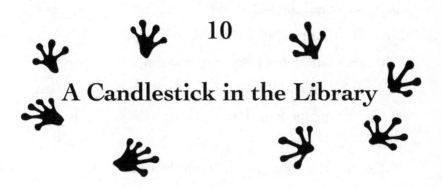

10

A Candlestick in the Library

$\mathcal{S}$ir Roderick held a thick scroll in front of him, as if presenting the king with a valuable jewel instead of a grim bit of parchment.

I shuddered at the sight of it.

We were gathered in the king's library. Queen Ermintrude settled herself and her skirts into the cushiest armchair close to the fire. Figgy claimed the only other armchair, next to his mother, pushing Angelica out of his way to get to it.

He wriggled into its cushions and gave Angelica a

smirk. His mother shone a beaming gaze over him as Lucy, her maid, darted about, arranging her mistress's skirts, fluffing the pillow behind her mistress's back, tucking a blanket over her mistress's lap.

With a rustle and a flourish, Sir Roderick unfurled the scroll over the length of the king's desk. The king pulled out his glasses and perched them on his nose.

Thistlewick stood by the door, head bowed.

Ulff blinked back tears. "She may have flung the gingerbread," he whispered, "but she used the right fork."

Angelica stared at her father, eyes pleading but voice silent.

Charming stood beside her, hand on her shoulder, the lucky mitten peeking from his gauntlet. He spied it, pulled it out, and tucked it into the sleeve of Angelica's gown. He looked up at the king and shook his head, the closest he would ever come to darting his father a glare. Then he pulled the woolen sock from his other gauntlet and gave it to the princess as well.

I closed my eyes. We'd done everything we knew to do.

And it hadn't worked.

"The contract, Your Majesty." With a flourish, Sir

Roderick set two small brass candlesticks on either side of the scroll. They cast a dim light over table and parchment.

The king leaned forward, forehead knotted into a frown. "I can barely read this. Where the devil is the candelabra?"

Thistlewick gave a small cough. "The good silver candelabra seems to have gone missing."

"Missing?" The king looked up. "Galloping goose feathers. Is nothing safe in this castle?" He let out a heavy sigh. "Very well. Do let's get on with it."

He pulled the contract near his face and held one of the candlesticks so close, I feared he would set both parchment and eyebrows ablaze. He squinted in the dim light and began reading.

"Hmmm," he said.

"Hunh," he said a moment later.

"Interesting," he said after that.

He came to a section dense with words and pulled the parchment closer still.

"Gifts and payments," he murmured, "to be sent to Queen Ermintrude in advance for the care and keeping of Princess Angelica." He looked up. "In advance? All of it?"

Sir Roderick spread his hands wide. "That *is* what the contract says, Your Majesty."

"Fine steeds do cost—*ow!*" Figbert flinched as his mother poked a sharp finger into his arm.

The king squinted at the parchment once more, candlelight casting a glow over the grooves and ridges of his brow. He *hmmm*ed and *hnph*ed, squinting harder as the words became smaller, then smaller still, until at last they were too small to read.

He looked up, blinking away the strain in his eyes. "Thistlewick?"

"Magnifying glass, Your Majesty." Thistlewick tipped his head. "I shall return with it quick as a wick."

As he strode from the room, Sir Roderick waved a hand.

"The rest is simply details," he said. "No need to waste time on it. Conditions, stipulations, restrictions, penalties, actions that constitute a breach. Basically the small print, which is why it is lettered in, well, small print."

Breach. That seemed a troublesome word. I searched my brain for its meaning and found none.

I leaned toward Charming. "Do we know what *breach* means?"

Charming narrowed his eyes. "Excellent question." He turned to Roderick. "What, sir, is a breach?"

"Yes." The king leaned forward. "I'd like to hear this, too."

Roderick waved his hand again. "It simply means that certain unlikely things could, should the aggrieved party choose to press the issue, change the terms of the contract. For example, if one party—you, for example, sire—were to, I don't know, somehow trick the queen into providing services above and beyond those listed—not that you ever would, of course—she could extract additional demands or void her obligations altogether. As I said, highly improbable. Inconceivable, one might say. Not worth the time to read, really, as Your Majesty would never do such a thing. We can seal the deal now, quickly and efficiently, with but a kiss."

The king frowned. "A kiss?" He shot a glance at Queen Ermintrude.

"Oh, not you, sire!" Roderick gave a thin little laugh. "Princess Angelica. And Prince Figbert. A simple kiss between the two of them, and the contract will be sealed forever, never to be broken."

"Who?" The king stared.

"What?" Charming frowned.

"Why?" I shook my head.

"No!" said Angelica. "I'm not old enough to kiss a boy. Especially not one I just met and can barely stand." She glared at Figbert. "It's *creepy* and *weird*."

"It is that," the king murmured, his brows still knotted.

Sir Roderick opened his mouth to speak, but at that moment, Thistlewick pushed back through the library door carrying a large, gold-handled magnifying glass.

Queen Ermintrude's eyes grew wide.

Figgy shot a glance at his mother.

Sir Roderick's Adam's apple bobbed in his throat.

"Sire," he said. "There's never anything truly important at the bottom of a contract. I hate to think of Your Majesty spending royal time on—"

The king flashed him a dark look. Roderick fell silent.

With the king wielding parchment and candle, and Thistlewick holding the glass steady, his Majesty read the contract aloud, every word. At the very end, in the tiniest script, he read:

This document seals the betrothal of His Royal Highness Prince Egbert and Her Royal Highness the Princess Angelica, forever and always in an unbreakable bond.

The king looked up, fury clouding his face. "Betrothal?"

Angelica frowned, confused. "Be*what*?"

"Be*trothal*." Queen Ermintrude clasped her hands together. "Isn't it wonderful? It will need to be a long engagement, of course, but eventually, you and my darling Figgy"—she turned a beaming gaze on her son—"will be married!"

The king pinned her with a thunderous glare. Charming stood speechless. Ulff and I shot each other horrified looks. Thistlewick nearly dropped the magnifying glass.

"*Married*?" Angelica stared at the queen, then at Figgy, then back at the queen. "That's even *more* creepy and weird. I'm not old enough to—"

"That's why it's a long engagement, dear," said the queen. "You won't be married until you *are* old enough."

"No." The king tossed the contract aside and thumped the candlestick onto the table. Its flame danced a wild flicker. "I'll never agree to this."

"Very wise, sire." Sir Roderick nodded. "Although"—he paused—"Angelica will no doubt marry one day, most likely a prince. She could certainly do worse than young Figbert, heir to a vast kingdom and, as the queen has pointed out, magnificent palace."

Figbert puffed his chest.

Ermintrude smiled sweetly at Angelica. "Yes." Her voice was a purr. "Just one little kiss, my dear, and our—er—*your* future will be secured."

"Never," said Angelica, her voice steady and low, which was somehow more alarming than when she shouted. "I will never, in any way, at any time, for any reason kiss Figgy. Or should I say *Froggy*, because I would rather kiss a frog."

As she spoke, the candles quivered, their flames flared. The light of them hurled trembling shadows above us on the walls.

Angelica paid no heed. She snatched her rounders ball from her gown, hiked her skirts, and stormed from the room. As she slammed the heavy oak door behind her, a great gust swept through the chamber. The draperies billowed. The parchment fluttered.

The candles flickered and went out.

11

A Queen in Dismay

When Thistlewick got the candles lit once more, the king was no longer seated at his desk. He stood before Queen Ermintrude, his face dark—so dark, the glow of the candlelight did not reach its darkest depths.

"Your trickery has done you no good," he told her. "Angelica will not be betrothed to Prince Figbert, now or in the future. I ask that you pack your trunks and leave my castle." He arched an eyebrow at Sir Roderick. "See that they do."

Roderick opened his mouth to reply, but when he

caught the full force of the king's fury roiling over the king's face, he closed it again.

Queen Ermintrude was not so easily silenced. "I can see my efforts here are not appreciated." She lifted her nose in the air. "If you wish your daughter to tear about the castle like an ill-mannered monkey, it's none of my affair. I will certainly not stay where I'm not wanted. I must, however, point out the very late hour."

She waved a hand toward the window. The sun had long since dipped below the castle's battlements, and the sky beyond the window shone black.

"I should hate to think you would throw any woman and child, let alone a queen and a prince—"

"And a maid," said her maid.

"—and a maid—yes, thank you, Lucy—out into such a dark and menacing night."

The king closed his eyes and pinched the knob of anger between his brows.

"Very well," he said. "Stay until morning. Then leave and never return."

Breakfast the next day was a merry affair, the merriest in my many days at the castle.

Rays of morning sun sliced through the breakfast

room windows, glinting off Charming's armor and casting a warm glow over platters of eggs, rolls, and sausages.

I hadn't yet heard Queen Ermintrude's carriage rumble from the courtyard, but the queen and her son had not come to breakfast.

The king sat in his place at the head of the table, Charming at his side. And for the first time since I'd known him, the knot of worry that usually bunched the king's forehead was gone.

As Ulff and I took our seats, my heart swelled with such merriness that I thought even one more pinprick of it would cause me to float from my chair. Charming had given up on stuffing porridge down everyone's throats, at least for the moment, and Ulff merrily piled a teetering stack of gingerbread on his plate.

Sir Roderick skulked in and filled a plate with bacon and a bit of egg. "Horrid headache," he said as he skulked back out.

"Licking his wounds, more like," muttered Ulff.

I nodded and shoveled a forkful of eggs in my mouth. I glanced across the table . . . and swallowed. In my merriment, I had not noticed that the seat across from mine was empty.

The king seemed to take notice at that same moment.

He glanced down the length of the table. "Has anyone seen Angelica?"

Ulff looked at me, I looked at him, we both looked at Charming, and we three of us shook our heads.

"Begging your pardon, sire." Thistlewick stepped forward. "One of the chambermaids heard Princess Angelica in her bedchamber this morning. She seemed to be talking to herself, but when the maid tapped lightly on her door to see if anything was amiss, the princess opened it a crack, poked her head out, and proclaimed everything to be fine."

The king considered this. "Did she seem fine?"

"The princess asked if Cook could send up a breakfast tray," said Thistlewick. "With extra chocolates."

The king raised his eyebrows. "She seems to have regained her appetite."

"I thought so, sire," said Thistlewick. "She told the maid she simply wanted to be by herself for a time."

"No doubt she does," said the king. "She ran off before she heard the queen was leaving, and I haven't had a chance to tell her. I should never have allowed that woman here in the first place." He dabbed his toast rather forcefully into a puddle of jam on his plate. "Thank you, Thistlewick. I'll have a talk with the princess."

Thistlewick bowed his head. "Very good, sire."

He turned to take his place at the door—

—and was barreled nearly flat by Queen Ermintrude. She swooped into the room, robes flying, skirts aswirl, crown ready to tumble from her head.

"Pardon me," Thistlewick rather gasped. He'd just managed to right himself—

—when the queen's maid hurtled past, cracking him well-nigh senseless with a jar of headache powders she was no doubt bringing for the queen.

"Madame!" The king rose to his feet. "Whatever is the matter?"

The queen swayed and sagged and grasped the back of a chair.

"It's Figgy!" she managed to choke out. "He's gone!"

12

A Pace on the Carpet

The servants searched the castle. The King's Men scoured the grounds. The assistant groom volunteered to swim the moat to see if Figbert had fallen in. The queen nearly passed out at the mention of water.

The queen's maid, not wanting to alarm her mistress further, slipped out to the garden while the queen slept, and prodded a stick into the depths of the lily pond. She gave the cattails a good shake while she was at it. And then she went and poked about the moat, just to be certain.

But neither she, nor the assistant groom, nor the castle servants or King's Men, found any sign of Figgy.

Charming insisted that he lead the wider search.

"I *am* the royal detective." He paced the length of the library, his armored feet *thunk-thunk*ing over the thick library rug. "I have business cards that say as much."

Sir Roderick raised a dark eyebrow. "For a coin, the village scribe will letter anything on a card."

The king had gathered us in his library to sort out what to do next. Queen Ermintrude had collapsed onto the king's chair, and the king had let her. Her maid Lucy spooned out a measure of headache powders and stirred them into the queen's tea.

Sir Roderick settled into the plush armchair

near the fire and sat with legs crossed, studying his fingernails. Ulff and I tucked ourselves close to a wall tapestry to keep out of the way of Charming's pacing. Ulff had brought along what was left of his breakfast gingerbread, wrapped in a napkin.

The king himself stood at the window, gazing over his lands. His hands were clasped behind his back, his face furrowed in thought.

Angelica still hunkered in her bedchamber, refusing to talk to any of us.

"I have the skills." Charming turned to *thunk* the other way. "With the aid of my noble assistant, Nobbin, and faithful guard, Ulff, I did discover what happened to the woodcutter's children."

"And the missing porridge," said Ulff.

"And the porridge." Charming stopped pacing and went to stand behind the king. "My men and I are well fit to find young Figbert. Send us out to investigate."

The king did not turn from the window. "You did well for the woodcutter," he said. "But this is dire."

"The woodcutter's children were dire," said Charming.

"And the porridge," said Ulff through a bite of gingerbread.

"And the—" Charming stopped. "Well, not the

porridge. But certainly the woodcutter's children, and this time we have a plan."

The king turned his head. "You do?"

Ulff gulped his gingerbread. "We do?"

Charming cut a look at me, and I nodded.

"We do," he said. "First—"

"We need to know why he's gone," I whispered.

"We'll work out the reason the young prince disappeared," said Charming. "To my mind, there are three possibilities."

The king tipped his head, listening.

"One—" Charming held up an armored finger.

"He ran away," I whispered.

"There is always the possibility that young Figbert ran away," said Charming.

"Ran away?" The queen held a hand to her chest as Lucy fluttered her mistress's face with a small fan. "Whatever would he run away *from*? I've given him everything he could possibly want, with the promise of more in the very near future. He would never run away."

"Well, then," said Charming, "two—" He held up a second finger.

"He got lost," I whispered.

"It is possible the lad strolled out for a walk and simply lost his way," said Charming.

"But Figgy doesn't go for walks." The queen wrinkled her brow. Her maid pressed a cold cloth to it. "And he certainly wouldn't do so *here*. Wherever would he go?"

"There are the castle grounds," said Charming.

"Which your King's Men have already searched," said the queen.

"Or the village," said Charming.

"The *village*!" The queen brushed aside Lucy's cloth and pressed her fingertip to her forehead. "Darling

Figgy would never step foot there. Not after the way the villagers mistreated him."

Mistreated? Ulff looked at me and raised a bristled eyebrow. I raised a brow back and shrugged.

"Or he could have gone to—" Charming stopped.

"The woods," said Ulff, helpfully.

"Woods?" The queen stared at him.

"Forest," said Charming.

"Trees," said Ulff. "It's where we went when we helped the bears."

The queen drew a sharp breath. "There are *bears* in your woods?" She collapsed back into the chair and Lucy lifted the teacup to her mouth.

"I wouldn't worry about them." Ulff waved the thought of the bears aside. "They're only after a bit of hot cereal. It's the wolves you have to look out for."

"Wolves?" The queen bolted upright.

"But they hardly ever bother anybody," said Ulff. He frowned. "Although they are fond of the color red. And piglets."

The queen lifted the shaky teacup. "And the last possibility?"

Charming held up a third armored finger. "Three—"

The queen waited, teacup halfway to her lips. Lucy

stopped her fanning and clutched the back of the chair.

"Someone took him," I whispered.

"We must consider," said Charming, "that Prince Figbert has been . . . kidnapped."

The queen gasped. Lucy let out a breath. Her shoulders sagged.

"But who would want to take my darling Figgy?" cried the queen.

"Nobody I can think of," Ulff muttered.

"Who would want to harm him?" she continued.

"Oh," said Ulff. "That's different."

"And wherever would they be keeping him?" said the queen.

"That, madame"—the king turned from the window and placed a hand on Charming's shoulder—"is precisely what the prince and his men will find out."

13

A List of Suspects

I wrote SUSPECTS at the top of the page and held my pencil at the ready.

We were in the stable again. Charming continued his pacing, this time clanking a path over the worn stone floor of the stable aisle, his helmet cradled in the crook of his arm.

"Who would take Prince Figbert?" he said. "And why?"

"Well." Ulff dug the napkin of gingerbread from his pocket. Darnell nickered, so Ulff broke off a plump bit of gingerbread and held it out to him. He bit off a good-sized chunk for himself. "There's no lack of folks who haven't taken kindly to the young prince," he said as he chewed. "He does know how to throw an insult."

Charming nodded. "That he does. We should write down everyone Prince Figbert has offended."

"It'd be quicker to write down everyone he *hasn't*," said Ulff.

"That would be a short list," I said.

"Wouldn't be any villagers on it, that's for sure," said Ulff.

"Villagers. Yes!" Charming turned. "The young prince was particularly unpleasant on our jaunt to Twigg. Who was the first villager insulted?"

"The butcher," Ulff blurted out in a gust of gingerbread crumbs. He wiped his face and brushed crumbs from his tunic. "Said he wouldn't step foot in the good man's shop."

I wrote BUTCHER on the list.

"And then the baker," said Ulff.

Charming nodded. "And the candlestick maker."

I wrote down BAKER and CANDLESTICK MAKER.

Charming narrowed his eyes. "And what of that peddler fellow?"

"Rumpelstiltskin?" said Ulff.

Charming gave a sharp nod. "That's the one."

Ulff frowned. "The young princeling tossed enough insults to cover near everyone." He gave his chin a brisk scratch. "But I don't remember Mr. Stiltskin sticking around long enough to get hit by one."

"No." Charming gave his new, now-bent plume a small tweak. "I suppose not." He sighed. "Is that it, then? Have we thought of everyone?"

I studied the list.

Suspects

1. Butcher
2. Baker
3. Candlestick Maker

"Maybe we should wait before we set off to pillage the village," I said.

Ulff gave a wise nod. "Twigg folk do get irked at pillaging."

"And none of them have motive," I said. "Figbert spent all that long morning insulting them. Why would one of them snatch him and bring him back for more?"

Ulff nodded again. "If you see a skunk, you don't take it home."

"Unless!" Charming held a finger in the air. "Unless they have something to gain by it."

"What would they gain?" I said.

"Riches," said Ulff. "They could be holding on to Figgy until the queen gives them payment. Are any of the villagers in need of coin?"

"Well, yes." I studied the list. "All of them. But if they kidnapped Figgy for coin, why haven't they sent the queen a ransom note?"

Ulff shrugged. "Maybe they aren't very good at it."

"Maybe." I took a breath. "But maybe we should look closer to home."

Charming stopped clanking again. "Closer to home? But Nobbin, we live in the castle. There's nothing close by but fields and the moat. And we've already checked the moat."

"I think he means closer than that." Ulff swallowed the last of his gingerbread. "I think he means the castle proper."

"The castle proper? But—great gosling, Nobbin! You can't think it one of us."

"Well." I swallowed. "Prince Figbert has been rude to nearly everyone here. The footmen, the maids—"

"And Cook," said Ulff. "He insulted her best soup."

"Cook?" Charming flung his armored hands wide. Darnell startled. "Cook is much too overburdened in the kitchens already. When would she find time to kidnap a prince?"

"Maybe she had help," said Ulff.

Charming looked at him. "From the kitchen maids?"

"From all of them," I said. "Maids, grooms, footmen."

"But to what end?" Charming stared at me.

I shrugged. "They may think to teach him a lesson. There's nothing vexes the castle staff more than a churlish houseguest."

Charming nodded. "They do hate bad manners." Then he shook his head. "But no. Thistlewick would have to be a party to it, and I simply can't think it of him."

This was the tricky part.

"I don't like to think it of him, either," I said. "But he might have the best motive of all."

Ulff had been digging in the napkin, plucking up crumbs. Now he stopped. He tilted his head. "Thistlewick is fond of the princess," he said.

"And"—Charming gave this thought a spin—"he might think getting rid of Prince Figbert would save her going off with the queen." He gave himself a shake. "But no. Not Thistlewick. I simply can't think it. We have other suspects to consider. There is, for example, the—ah—witch! Yes. Prince Figbert did spit out her gingerbread."

"But," said Ulff, "that lovely woman wasn't there to see him do it."

"No. Maybe not," said Charming. "But these things do get back. Twigg folk like to talk."

Ulff raised a brow. "Not to the witch. She's made it so they're afraid of her."

"Yes." Charming thought about this. "And even if she did take him, I can't see her tolerating him for long. Irksome as he is, she'd soon send him back to the castle."

"That's the problem with all our suspects. They'd

every one of them send him back. Unless—" I had a new thought. "Unless the culprit is someone as irksome as Figgy."

Charming frowned. "So we're back to Stiltskin again?"

"Or Figbert's mother." Ulff thought about this and shook his head. "No. That doesn't seem right. She's the one reported him missing in the first place."

"Not his mother, nor Stiltskin." I took a breath. "I was thinking of Sir Roderick."

"Roderick?" Charming frowned. "But he's my father's cousin. And closest advisor."

"He's also the spit-wattled wastrel what convinced our fine king to let the queen into the castle to begin with," said Ulff. "And that toady little prince with her."

Charming turned this thought over.

"But we're talking of a child," he said. "A nettlesome, tedious child, to be sure. With terrible taste in soup. But I can't think Roderick would tear even that sort of child from his mother."

Ulff gave a snort. "It didn't worry him overmuch when Hansel and Gretel were torn from Mr. and Mrs. Woodcutter."

Charming raised his eyebrows. "It didn't, did it?"

"And"—Ulff's nostrils widened, as if he had gotten a whiff of the foulness that was Sir Roderick—"he's the one pushing for Angelica to be torn from her father. And from us."

I nodded. "And he was not well pleased when the king ordered the queen and her son from the castle. Might he have stashed the prince away to stop them leaving?"

"To give him time to convince my father," Charming said slowly.

He looked at me.

"Nobbin," he said, "you've finally landed a suspect we can agree on."

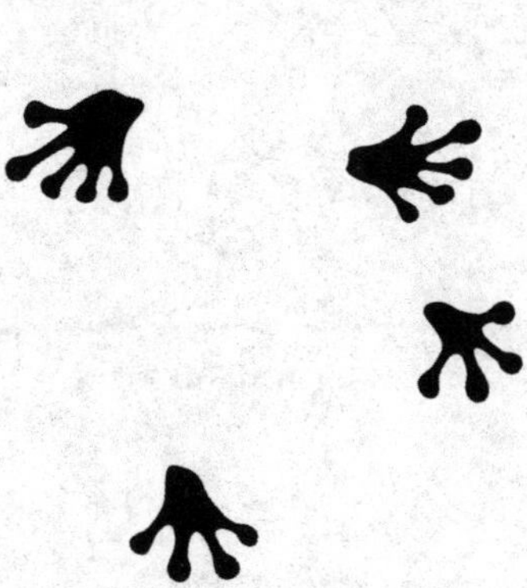

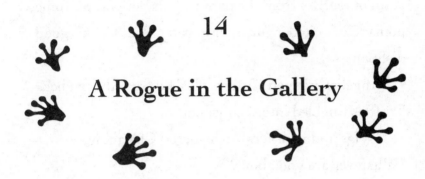

14

A Rogue in the Gallery

$\mathfrak{W}$e scuttled across the courtyard and into the side door of the castle. Our thought was to ferret out Sir Roderick without him knowing and watch his movements from the shadows.

We crept down the passage toward the stairs with our heads cocked back to make sure Cook didn't prowl from the kitchens—

—and ran nearly smack into Angelica.

Or she nearly ran smack into us.

She was tottering toward the stairway carrying a stack of household goods higher

115

than her head. A plush pillow from the drawing room. A tin of truffles from the pantry. Oils, lotions, perfumes, pomades. A pitcher filled with water. And Cook's good dishpan.

Angelica jumped. Water sploshed from the pitcher. Truffles tumbled into the dishpan.

"Wigs and whiskers!" whispered Charming. "Whatever are you about?"

"I wanted chocolate," said Angelica.

To prove it, she fished a truffle from the dishpan and popped it in her mouth.

"It makes me feel better," she mumbled around the truffle. She narrowed her eyes at Charming, daring him to disagree.

"You *have* been through a lot." Charming sighed. "I might well drown my sorrows in chocolate as well. Here." He reached for the dishpan. "Let me carry it for you."

"No." Angelica spun sideways, pulling the dishpan from his reach. "I can do it myself."

"Very well." Charming stood aside, and Angelica stomped up the stairs toward her bedchamber.

We climbed up after her on softer feet. We slipped through passages and down hallways till we reached the drawing room. The door was cracked slightly. We peered in.

"I don't see anything," Ulff whispered.

"Me, neither," I said.

"Nor I," agreed Charming.

We checked the ballroom and the dining room and drawing room. We checked the throne room and even the king's library. We gave thought to checking Thistlewick's sitting room, then thought better of it. Thistlewick and Roderick were like similar ends of two magnets, pushing each other apart. Roderick would not enter the butler's apartments.

We peeked in storerooms and the laundry, dodging servants and King's Men as we wound our way through passages.

We finally spied Sir Roderick in the gallery overlooking the great hall. We slipped into the gallery unseen and took up watch behind one of the thick marble columns.

"What is he doing?" Ulff hissed.

I pressed my back to the hard column and peered around its curve. Charming peered around its other side.

Sir Roderick stood near the gallery rail, well back

enough not to be seen by anyone looking up from the hall. He stretched his head forward to look over the rail, eyes darting this way and that. He stalked the length of the rail, scanning the hall below, then stepped back into the shadows.

Charming and I pulled our heads back at the same moment.

"I believe you're right, Nobbin," Charming whispered. "He does seem suspicious."

Ulff scrunched his face. "But is it *suspicious* suspicious? Or just his everyday suspicious?"

It was a fair point. Sir Roderick seemed to skulk about wherever he went, even when the skulking wasn't needed.

"Too early to tell, I fear," said Charming.

We peered around the column once more, this time Ulff taking a spot crouched below me.

118

Sir Roderick had now pulled the contract from his robes. He seated himself on a stone bench at the far end of the gallery, where a shaft of light shone through a window. He scrolled the contract out onto the bench beside him, angled to catch the light.

He ran his finger down the script, muttering to himself as he read.

"The party of the first part . . ." Roderick muttered. "Yes. Yes. Yes." His finger skipped down the scroll. "The kiss must be between Prince Figbert and— yes, yes, I know that part. Oh! If either party has previously—no, that doesn't apply. Ah, here."

He lifted the parchment to the light.

"The kiss will seal the contract"—his voice rang out through the gallery, easy for we spies to hear—"whether said kiss is purposeful or by chance."

Sir Roderick gave a slow nod, rescrolled the scroll, and slipped it back into his robes. He pressed his hands together and tapped them against his lips.

"By chance." He raised an eyebrow. "That should be easy to arrange. Our dear princess tends to lunge when provoked. I need only place Prince Figbert in the path of her lunging. With lips puckered." His mustache curled into a menacing smile. "And as luck would have it, I seem to have a bit more time to arrange things perfectly."

He rose to his feet, tipped another quick glance over the rail, then stalked through the doorway at the far end. The heavy door banged shut behind him, echoing down the length of the gallery.

We three of us sank down to the floor.

Ulff shook his head. "That worm's-breath scroundrel is trying to trick our Princess Angelica into the kiss."

"And says luck has given him more time." Charming narrowed his eyes. "I'll wager that luck's name is Sir Roderick."

I nodded. "He's stashed Figbert away somewhere until he can arrange things."

"We should tell the king," said Ulff.

Charming frowned. "To what end? My father will think we've confused something overheard. While we were purposely listening. My father holds no affection for eavesdropping."

"And if he did believe us," I said, "and asked Sir Roderick—"

"He would simply deny it," said Charming.

Ulff nodded. "And laugh in our faces, most like."

"So." Charming rose to his feet. "We must find more proof."

"Or," I said, "find Prince Figbert."

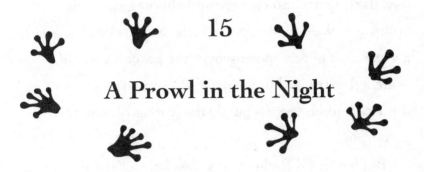

15

A Prowl in the Night

I slipped through the passageway and took my position across from Sir Roderick's chambers.

A window was cut into the thick stone wall behind me. It was framed by heavy draperies and had a wide wooden sill. I climbed onto the sill, slid behind the drapery, and pulled my knees to my chest. A full moon hung low in the sky, throwing a soft glow onto the floor of the hall.

We had agreed, Charming, Ulff, and I, that we could only find proof—or Figbert—by following Sir Roderick to see where he went and what he did.

We had followed him about the castle all the long day, darting around corners and slipping through archways. We'd learned very little. Sir Roderick spent a great deal of time poring over the parchment. He snatched extra pudding from the footman's tray at dinner. And he spent a particularly long time in the garderobe.

But we could find nothing that led to Prince Figbert.

"If you had something to hide," Charming finally asked, "where would you hide it?"

"Sock drawer," said Ulff. "That's where I hide my doodads and whatnots."

"Yes," said Charming. "But I fear it unlikely Roderick has stashed the young prince in with his socks."

I had been turning a thought in my mind. "I think we have the question wrong," I said. "It's not *where* Sir Roderick would hide something, but *when*. If you wanted to do something without anyone to see, when would you do it?"

Charming thought about this. "At night."

Ulff's eyes grew wide. "When folks are asleep."

We divided up the hours of the night to watch

Sir Roderick's chambers in turn.

My turn was first.

I shifted on the hard wooden sill. I'd been here some time and had heard nothing save an occasional grunting snore muffled by the thick wood door of Sir Roderick's bedchamber. I'd seen even less.

I shifted again. My eyes felt heavy, and my stomach growled. I leaned my head against the coolness of the window glass.

I started awake moments later. I glanced out the window. I must have slept sometime more than I'd thought, for the moon was now high in the sky.

I flexed my shoulders and rubbed sleep crust from my eyes.

And spied movement in the garden below.

It was Angelica. She had refused to leave her bedchamber for dinner, but now here she was, nigh midnight, prowling through the grass.

I pressed my face to the glass and watched.

She held a small net in one hand and a crockery jar in the other. She took one long, sneaking step, then another, like a tiger stalking prey. With a flick of a wrist, she gave the net a quick swish, then held it up to the moonlight.

Inside the net, three fireflies darted about, their lights pulsing in a brilliant glow.

Angelica pulled the lid from the jar, dumped the fireflies inside, and stoppered the jar back up again.

Then she set off through the grass, hunting more fireflies.

16

A Surprise on a Pillow

id you observe anything suspicious?"

I bolted upright and blinked to keep my eyes open.

We were at breakfast. Thistlewick was at his post by the door, but the king nor anyone else had come down yet. I'd nearly nodded off in my porridge.

Charming was leaning across the table, gaze fixed on Ulff and me.

Ulff shook his head. "Not a thing. Of course, I may have dozed for a minute or two. Or three."

Charming turned to me.

"Well, I—"

I thought of Angelica, stalking fireflies in the garden. That was surely suspicious. But it was not what Charming was asking.

"I didn't see or hear Sir Roderick do anything," I said.

"Nor did I." Charming sat back. "He's a sticky wicket."

Clattering footsteps echoed from the passageway. "You know she can't control herself." The queen's voice barreled into the breakfast room before the queen herself did. "It's why you sent for me in the first place."

We looked up.

Queen Ermintrude burst through the door, her skirts an angry swirl. The king strode in after her, eyes blazing, jaw clenched till the very skin of it had turned white. Thistlewick leaped back to stop being flattened by them. Lucy bustled in a few moments later, cold cloth held at the ready.

The king stopped at his place at the head of the table. He gripped the back of his chair and spoke through still-clenched teeth.

"Angelica may not know which fork to use or how to sit the way you think proper or how to hold her temper when sorely, sorely provoked," he told the queen. His voice was a growl. "But that is a far cry from *kidnapping*."

Charming's mouth snapped open. "Kidnapping?"

Ulff and I shot glances at each other.

The king shook his head. "Her Majesty has convinced herself your sister has somehow taken Prince Figbert."

Charming knotted his brow. "Angelica is but a small girl. How would she manage it?"

The queen's mouth stretched into a horrifying smile. "I'm so glad you asked. She could not do it—alone. The little princess clearly had help."

She swung her gaze toward Thistlewick, who stood at the doorway, staring straight ahead.

Charming pulled back his head. "Not—"

Rage filled the king's face. "You can't mean—"

"I *do* mean," she said. "Your butler."

"Please." Charming pressed his face against the wood plank of the door. "If you know anything, you have to tell us."

"Go away." Angelica's voice was muffled.

"I understand if you don't want to talk to us," said Charming. "But why won't you talk to Father?"

Angelica said nothing for a moment. Then she hissed

something that sounded like, "Just be quiet."

Charming frowned. "What?"

"Just *because*, okay?" Angelica snapped.

Charming sighed.

"People are starting to think you're hiding something," he said. "They're wondering if maybe Queen Ermintrude is right."

"They can think what they like."

"Perhaps. But Queen Ermintrude now says Thistlewick must be in on it."

Silence.

Then: "Thistlewick?"

Charming swallowed. "Ermintrude thinks he meant to protect you. She's urging Father to toss him in the dungeon."

"The dungeon?" Angelica's voice had grown louder. She sounded to be just on the other side of the door now.

We heard a click, then a clank, then the wood door creaked open a sliver.

Angelica's face appeared in the crack. "Truly?"

Charming nodded.

Angelica's face disappeared. The door groaned wide.

Charming glanced over his shoulder at us, then stepped inside. Ulff and I scuttled in after him.

Angelica stood beside her bed in the middle of her bedchamber. Standing there, next to thick bedposts hung with heavy, woven draperies, her head bent and her hands clasped, the princess looked very small.

"Angelica." Charming took a step toward her. "We need to puzzle out what really happened. We need to find Prince Figbert."

She nodded.

She took a breath.

"Well," she said. "You found him."

She reached up and pulled back the draperies.

Sitting on the princess's plump royal pillow was an enormous green frog.

17

A Princess in a Pickle

$\mathfrak{T}$he frog blinked.

"Ah!" Ulff jumped back.

I confess, I jumped a bit with him.

Ulff slowly leaned forward and peered at the frog. "It's *real.*"

Angelica sighed. "I know."

"So." Charming angled himself sideways, stretched an arm, and gave the frog's smooth green skin a quick jab with his armored finger. "You believe this frog to be Prince Figbert?"

"He *is* Prince Figbert," said Angelica.

Charming frowned. "How do you know?"

Angelica blew out an exasperated breath. "He *told* me." She crossed her arms over her chest. "I never should have shown him to you. I knew you'd be like this."

Charming straightened. He looked hurt. "Like what?"

A voice echoed through the room: "Like an overgrown tin can who never stops talking."

The voice was low.

Gravelly.

And did not come from Angelica.

We stared at the frog.

He stared back. His wide frog mouth stretched wider into . . . a wide frog smile.

Charming blinked. "But who—what—*how*—"

"—did this happen?" finished the frog. Froggy. Figgy. He rolled his bulging frog eyes. "*She* knows." He motioned a foot—paw? flipper?—toward Angelica.

"That may be," said Charming, "but *we*, my fine young . . . frog, do not. Pray, tell us."

Figgy gave a frog sigh, which sounded more like a growly burp. "The night all of this"—he flicked a bulgy-eyed look at his bulgy frog body—"happened,

138

I felt queasy after dinner. Not surprising, considering the dreck this castle calls food. I took to my bed and insisted my mother's maid bring me cocoa and a blanket. I woke at midnight feeling a bit better, but with a strong urge to lounge on a lily pad."

"Lily pad?" Charming frowned. "Did you not find that odd?"

The frog pulled himself up to his full, very short frog height.

"The lily pad," he said, "is my family's royal crest."

"Oh!" I looked at Ulff.

"*That's* what the fat round leaf is on their carriage."
Ulff shook his head. "I knew it had to be something."

"I went down to the garden pond, hoping to enjoy
a little peace and quiet," said Figgy. "And who should
be there but her." He flipped his foot at Angelica again.
"Bouncing her ball off the garden wall, over and over
and over. Until it finally bounced into the pond."

"If you hadn't hopped out from nowhere and scared
the very spit out of me," said Angelica, "I wouldn't have
thrown it so hard. Or so crooked."

The frog sighed. "The main thing is that the ball
landed in the pond. And the princess thought I should
get it out for her." He stretched his froggy smile again.
"So I did. But that's when I caught my reflection in the
pond."

"He shrieked," said Angelica. "Or . . . croaked."

"As would anyone," said Figgy. "I was noticeably
smaller, rounder, and much, much greener. In short—
literally—I was a frog."

Charming frowned at Angelica. "But why is he
here?"

"He followed me back," said Angelica. "And
wouldn't leave."

Charming shook his head. "Simply carry him—and that pillow, for you shan't want to sleep on it again—back to his own bedchamber. He can't be that heavy."

Angelica slumped against the bed. "I can't," she said. "Or he'll hop away and tell his mother. And she'll tell our father. And if Father banished me for accidentally throwing a ball at Darnell, what will he do to me for"—she flung a hand toward Figgy—"this?"

Ulff shook his head in confusion. "It's not *your* fault he's a frog."

"It most certainly is," said Figgy. "Do you not remember? In the library? She called me Froggy and said that's what she'd rather kiss—a frog. She spelled me."

Ulff looked at Angelica in wonder. "You can cast spells?"

"Of course she can't." Charming waved away the thought. "She has no more magic than you do, Ulff. She did not turn him into a frog."

"But what if I did?" Angelica looked up at Charming, eyes wide. "I was sorely vexed that night. What if I was *so* vexed that it bubbled up and burst into magic, just in that instant? What if my vex turned into a hex?"

Ulff thought about this. "The candles *did* flicker and blaze. And poof out."

"As I so reminded her," said Figgy. "She turned me this way. Now she must turn me back."

He puckered his wide, smooth, slippery frog lips (which did not look so much different from the lips he had when he was a prince), closed his round, bulbous, bulging frog eyes (again, not much different from his prince eyes), leaned toward Angelica, and—

"No!" She clamped a hand over her mouth.

Ulff shuddered. "What is he doing?"

"I think," I said, "he wants a kiss. It's the customary way to break a frog spell."

Angelica shook her head. "I can't do it," she said through still-clamped hands.

"Of course you can't," said Charming. "The royal lips of a princess should never touch any part of a frog."

"It's not that." Angelica pulled her hands away a slight bit so she could talk. "If I could just give him a quick kiss and turn him back into his normal horrible self so he and his mother would leave the castle for good, I'd do it. In the flicker of an eyelash. But if I kiss him—"

I narrowed my eyes. "You seal the contract."

Angelica nodded. "And no one can unseal it."

18

A Whisper in the Stairwell

orry not." Charming tipped Angelica's chin up with an armored finger. "You could not have spelled Frog—er—*Fig*bert. But we shall find out who did and demand they reverse the magic."

The princess had been slumped against her bed. Now she stood upright.

"I'll go with you," she said.

"And leave me by myself?" croaked Figgy. "With no one to fetch my chocolates and exfoliate my feet?"

Ulff stared at Angelica. "He makes you . . . ?

She gave a grim nod. "And rub them with lotion."

A shudder shook the bristles of Ulff's whole body.

A shudder ran the length of me, too.

"Although." Figgy dragged this word out in a long, ratchety croak. He flicked a bulgy-eyed look at Angelica. "I suppose I could find someone else to fetch them for me."

His thin frog lips stretched into a horrid frog smile.

Angelica dug her fists into the folds of her skirt.

Charming placed his armored hands on her shoulders. "I never believed I could say these words, but Prince Figbert is right. You need to stay here, keep him quiet, keep him from hopping away, and keep the chambermaids from laying eyes on him."

"And," said Ulff, "keep your lips far, far, far from his." He gave another shudder.

Angelica gave a sigh.

Charming gave her shoulders an encouraging squeeze.

"Be brave," he said.

He turned smartly on his armored heel, and the three of us—Prince Charming, Ulff, and me—slipped from Angelica's bedchamber.

Charming clanked off down the passageway. Ulff and I scuttled behind.

"So." Ulff's legs pumped double-quick to keep up

with Charming's long strides. "Where is it we're going with such purpose?"

"We, my fine fellow," Charming said over his shoulder, "are going—"

He stopped. Ulff very nearly slammed into Charming's shiny backplate, and I very nearly slammed into Ulff.

Charming turned to me. "Where are we going, Nobbin?"

"Well . . ."

I started to reach in my tunic for paper and pencil to make a list. It seemed that was my answer to everything these days. But I'd made so many lists of late, I feared I hadn't a scrap of clean paper left. I let my hand drop to my side.

"We need to think." I lowered my voice lest someone chanced to be lurking nearby. "Who would have the skill to spell the prince? Or the opportunity? And how did they spell him?"

As we gave this thought, Charming set off again.

"I still vote for Sir Roderick," Ulff whispered. "Just because Figgy's a frog instead of a regular kidnapped prince doesn't mean Sir Roderick isn't the mangy scab behind it."

Charming shook his head. "I've known Roderick my whole life. I've spent nearly every day of it in his presence. And Roderick's never shown the least sign of magic."

I thought about this. "And he would be one to use it at every occasion if he could." I frowned. "Has anyone shown sign of magic in the castle? Or in the village?"

We slipped into the round stairwell and began tip-tapping our way down the stone steps.

"None of the servants seem magical," whispered Ulff. "Nor villagers, either."

Charming gave a grim nod. "But for that Stiltskin fellow. He seems to have a magical way of conjuring into his pocket whichever bit or bob catches his fancy."

"That'd be more trickery than sorcery," said Ulff.

"And theft," said I.

"True." Charming sighed. "What is wrong with this kingdom? I always thought it a magical place, what with our dwarfs and our castle and our troll. We even call our patch of wood the Enchanted Forest—a bit optimistically it seems, since here we are with a frogged prince, and we can't think of even one person—"

He stopped.

"—who can—"

He stopped again.

"—enchant things. Hold on." He held up an armored hand.

We came to a complete standstill in the middle of the curved stairs.

"Aside from bears and wolves, the forest also has"—Charming looked at us—"a witch. Witches," he said, "cast spells."

"That lovely woman?" Ulff shook his head. "I'll never believe it of her."

"Nor I." I chewed my lip. "Though she did deliver the gingerbread for the queen's arrival." I shook my head. "But that doesn't make sense. Figbert can't have been the only one affected by it. Near everyone in the castle ate it. If the gingerbread were spelled, we'd *all* be frogs."

"I'd be eight frogs and a tadpole all by myself," said Ulff.

"And," I said, "she sent the gingerbread before she knew Figbert would insult it."

Charming sighed. "I suppose you're right. It's

unlikely she's the spell-caster."

He turned to tread once more down the steps. Ulff turned to follow.

I stayed where I was, thinking.

"But," I said.

They stopped and looked up at me.

"She may *know* something of frog spells," I said. "How the spell is cast. And who might have the power to cast it."

Charming narrowed his eyes. "She may at that."

He lifted his chest, slid his broken-plumed helmet onto his head, and turned.

"To the woods!" he said.

19

A Dash of Newt

𝕮*lunk.*

Clank.

"Hunf."

The royal groom hoisted Prince Charming onto Darnell.

The prince spurred Darnell to action.

"To the woods!" he cried.

Darnell turned and ambled down the hill toward Twigg. Ulff and I ambled along at his side. Charming swayed in the saddle, the leather creaking under his armor.

153

We clopped down the roadway and through the village, stopping only when we reached the edge of the forest. Charming swung from the saddle—and onto his backplate once again. Ulff and I helped him to his feet, and Charming plucked a leaf from his elbow guard, took up Darnell's reins, and led us through the woods.

"Ho!" He held up an armored hand once we reached the clearing.

No matter how many times I'd seen the the witch's cottage, my eyes still popped at the wonder of it. Gingerbread walls. Gingerbread doors. Gingerbread shutters. All of it sprinkled with sugar and held together with frosting. The sweet, spicy scent of it rolled over us like a frosted gingerbread cloud.

Guurrauwwwk.

The rumble of Ulff's stomach echoed through the clearing.

The witch must have heard, for Ulff had no more than clapped a hand to his belly when the gingerbread door swung open on its licorice hinges, and she stepped onto the gingerbread plank porch.

"Well." She brushed a dusting of flour from her cheek. "Isn't this a—" She frowned. "I'd like to say surprise, but I suppose it's not. What brings you to the dark heart of the forest?"

Charming tied Darnell to the candy cane porch rail, then turned to her. "We have something to tell you. Well, ask you, really. But before we do, you must promise to reveal it to no one."

The witch leveled a gaze at him. "I know how to keep secrets. Besides"—she spread her arms toward the wall of trees that towered about her cottage—"who would I tell?"

"Excellent!" Charming nodded. "It's what I hoped you'd say. "

He rubbed his armored hands together and told her about the frog.

When he finished, she frowned. "But why are you telling me all of this?"

Confusion wrinkled Charming's brow. "You're a witch. And the prince has been spelled."

She crossed her arms and cocked her head to one side. "And you think I spelled him."

"What? No!" Charming brushed this thought off with a wave of a shiny armored hand. "Not at all.

155

I never thought—"

Darnell snorted.

"Well, yes." Charming gave a little cough. "It did cross my mind. At first. But Nobbin here pointed out how unlikely it was you could have pulled it off—"

"Really?" The witch turned her narrow-eyed gaze at me.

I held up my hands. "That's not what I said." I could feel the slow burn crawling up my face. "I simply pointed out that, while you personally would never do such a thing"—leastways I hoped she wouldn't, since she was looking at me now with such fire, I feared she might well *poof!* me into a cinder at any moment—"you could help us find out who did."

The witch studied me, then turned back to Charming. "So first you suspect me, and now you want my help?"

He brightened. "Yes. You've got the picture entirely."

She looked at him for a long moment.

"Fine," she said. "What is it you want to know?"

Charming shot a glance at me.

"*Who*," I whispered, "and *how*."

"Yes." He turned back to the witch. "Do you have any idea who might have the skill, cunning, knowledge, and power to cast such a spell?"

The witch raised her eyebrows. "In these parts?" She shook her head. "Unless someone has recently stumbled upon magic they never before possessed, there's none I can think of."

Charming turned to Ulff and me. "You see?" He flung a hand in the air. "This truly *isn't* the magical kingdom I thought it to be."

"It really isn't," said the witch.

"Well." Charming let out a heavy breath. "I guess that's that, then. We journeyed this way for naught."

He reached for Darnell's bridle. Darnell tossed his head.

Charming frowned. "What—?"

"There's still the *how* of it," I told him.

Charming blinked. "The *how*. Yes!" He turned to the witch. "If someone did have the skill to frog a prince, how exactly would they frog him? A rhyming chant? The wave of a wand? Some sort of charm?"

"A potion," said the witch.

"Potion?" Charming pulled his head back.

I furrowed my brow. "What goes in it?"

The witch began naming ingredients. I scrambled in my tunic for paper and pencil.

"They'd most likely start with the basics," she said. "Eye of newt and toe of frog. Then it's really up to the spell-caster to decide what's best. Pond water most likely. The more pond scum you can scoop up with it, the better. The juice from the heart of a lily pad. A bit of mugwort perhaps, the kind used to season meats. It aids in stomach upset. There's a lot of moving around in a spell like this. Arms turn to legs, fingers to toes. Eyes move to the top of the head."

Ulff shook his head. "That would make me seasick." His eyes widened. "Figgy said he felt sick."

Charming narrowed his eyes. "He did indeed."

The witch nodded. "Mugwort relieves that to a small

degree. I might also add a pinch of cinnamon and sugar."

Ulff blinked. "For stomach upset?"

"To cover the taste," said the witch. "Although you can never really cover the bitterness of frog toe. Then mix it all in a bowl of the purest silver and heat with a candle of the deepest green until it thickens and starts to bubble."

Charming frowned. "And that's it?"

The witch nodded. "That's it."

Charming sighed. Then he looked up. "I don't suppose you could reverse such a spell?"

The witch shook her head. "A reverse depends entirely on what was put in the potion to begin with. And what conditions the caster placed on it, how it can be broken, that sort of thing."

"But we could try, surely," said Charming.

"I wouldn't," said the witch. "It's dangerous. A reverse spell when you don't know the original spell would likely make the first spell worse. It could keep it from being broken at all."

"So if you didn't frog him," said Ulff, "you can't unfrog him?"

"Not with a spell," said the witch.

Charming paced back and forth. "We're no closer

than we were. Pond scum. Cinnamon. Frog toe." He shook his head. "We know not enough to know where to go next."

I studied the list in my hand. "I'm not sure that's true," I said.

I scuffled in my tunic and brought out another list. I held the two lists up side by side.

Suspects

1. Butcher
2. Baker
3. Candlestick Maker

Potion

1. Eye of newt
2. Toe of frog
3. Pond water—scummy is best
4. Lily pad juice
5. Mugwort—for stomach ailment and to season meat
6. Cinnamon
7. Sugar
8. Silver bowl
9. Green candle

"We know exactly where to go," I said.

20

A Pinch of Cinnamon

To the—!"

Charming glanced at me.

"Village," I said.

"To the village!" cried Charming.

He took up Darnell's reins, snapped a crisp wave of farewell to the witch, and strode off toward the woods. Ulff and I scrambled to catch up, Ulff casting a disappointed glance over his shoulder at the thought of leaving all that home-baked goodness.

As we picked our way around the gnarled roots and fallen logs on the forest path, I pointed out the

likenesses between the two lists—our original list of suspects and the frog spell ingredients the witch had mentioned.

"Here." I pointed to the suspect list. "The butcher," I said. "He sells meat."

Charming shot an exasperated look at me over his shoulder. "Of course he does, Nobbin. That's why he's called a butcher."

Darnell blew out a long, shuddering horse breath.

Ulff leaned toward me and studied the two lists. "Hey!" He poked a sausage finger at an ingredient. "Mugwort. It seasons meats."

"Mugwort." Ahead of us, Charming's broken plume bobbed in agreement. "The butcher. Of course."

"And then there's the baker," I said.

Charming tipped his head. "With her many fine ingredients," he said slowly.

"Many fine *sweet* ingredients," said Ulff. "Sugar, for one. And cinnamon."

"I see how she may connect, yes," said Charming. "Pray continue."

"And last," I said, "the candlestick maker."

"Who fashions items made of silver—and candles." Charming and the plume gave a sharp nod.

"That takes care of a whole chunk of spell ingredients right there," said Ulff. "You think one of these villagers is the one what frogged the prince?"

"It could be, Ulff," said Charming. "It very well could be."

By this time, we'd reached the edge of the wood. The village lay beyond. Charming straightened his plume as well as it would straighten and clicked his tongue at Darnell.

"Come," he said. "We have a butcher to question."

We made our way down the lane to the butcher shop. Charming tied Darnell to a lamppost, and the prince, Ulff, and I went inside.

The butcher was behind his counter, wielding an enormous, glinting meat cleaver high above a beef roast. He gave one great *whack*, then glanced up from the cleaver, which looked to be stuck fast in the wooden butcher block.

He raised his eyebrows in surprise. "Your Highness!" He gave a quick bow. "What brings you here?"

"Well. Ah . . ." Charming darted a glance around the shop.

Ulff darted a panicked glance at me. We had thought *who* to question, but we had not thought what question to question them *with*. *"Have you perchance frogged our visiting prince?"* somehow didn't seem right.

"I come at the request of our castle cook," Charming said finally.

"Cook?" The butcher's eyebrows near popped from his forehead. "She usually sends a kitchen maid. Why would Your Royal Highness be running errands for the cook?"

"Yes. Well. I happened to be journeying this way," said Charming, "and offered my help. The kitchen staff is sorely taxed these days, what with the, ah, recent arrival of guests."

"The guests." The butcher nodded in sympathy. "And a finicky lot they are, too."

"Finicky, yes," said Charming. "You have the right of it there, my good butcher. Which is why I'm here. Because of the finickiness. Cook needs to know how you season your meats."

Ulff looked at me in surprise. I shook my head in wonder. The prince was a much better liar than I'd given him credit for.

"Is it with, perhaps," said Charming, "mugwort?"

The three of us—Charming, Ulff, and I—leaned forward to better hear the answer.

The butcher frowned. "I usually season with simple salt, but if it's mugwort Cook needs, I'd be glad to give it to her. I keep a bit here."

He opened a cupboard, frowned, then opened another. He shook his head and began pulling out drawers and bins. Finally, he stopped and scratched his head.

"I had mugwort," he said. "But it's missing."

"Missing," said Charming. "One of the very ingredients for the spell—and it's missing."

He untied Darnell, and we traipsed toward the next shop. Darnell's hooves clopped over the cobblestones, while Charming's armored feet clanked.

Clop.

Clank.

Clop.

Clank.

Ulff pointed down the lane. "Is that Rumpelstiltskin?"

I looked up. It was indeed the village peddler. He sauntered past the tailor shop, the pots and forks inside his coat clinking and swaying with each step.

"He's always trading for something," said Ulff. "He could have a frog toe stashed in that great galumphing coat of his, and no one would be the wiser."

"He could at that." Charming waved an armored hand high in the air. "I say!" he called out. "Mr. Stiltskin! May we have a word?"

Stiltskin darted a look over his shoulder, then jangled into an alleyway.

Charming dropped his hand. "I daresay we'll catch up to him sooner or later."

Darnell snorted.

We had arrived at the next shop. Charming tied Darnell's reins to the lamppost, and we pushed through the shop door.

A little bell jangled against the glass, and the smell of fresh-baked muffins swirled about us in a sweet, warm hug. I closed my eyes and breathed it in. It had a spicy bouquet, nutty with a delicate fruitiness and an underlying note of butter. I grew near dizzy from the scent of it.

I opened my eyes to see Ulff, eyes also closed, sagging toward me in a swoon, a look of pure bakery joy on his face.

I tipped him upright.

The baker woman scurried from the back of the shop, wiping her hands over her dough-caked apron.

She beamed at Charming. "Back so soon, Your Highness? Are you needing some sweets for the castle?"

"Yes!" said Ulff.

Charming raised an eyebrow at him. "No," he said.

"Not this moment. I was wondering more about sugar."

"Sugar?" The baker frowned.

Charming nodded. "And cinnamon."

"Sugar and cinnamon." The baker looked at him. "I do have a few cinnamon buns left."

She reached into the bakery case and pulled out a tray. Two sad-looking cinnamon buns rather drooped in the center of it.

"If I'd known you were coming, I could have made more. Although"—she gave a trembling smile—"they would not be cinnamon. I have stockpiles of sugar, although some of it does look to be gone. But every bit of my cinnamon, it seems, has been pinched."

"Pinched?" Charming's eyes grew wide.

"Stolen," she said.

Charming thanked her and we left. But not before Ulff gave her a coin for a basket of her muffins.

"Investigating does make a body hungry," he said.

"Cinnamon." Charming shook his head. "And sugar. Two more ingredients on our list gone missing."

We clop-clanked the length of the high street, nibbling muffins.

I spied Mr. Stiltskin again. But the moment I

spotted him, he spotted us. He clinked around a corner and disappeared.

Charming tied Darnell to the lamppost outside the candlestick shop and led the way inside.

The candlestick maker was perched on a ladder, dusting his wares.

"Your Highness!" He scrambled down.

"My good candlestick maker." Charming tipped his head. "I wonder," he said, "what have you here in silver?"

"Ah, well." The candlestick maker turned to the shelf he'd been dusting. "I have silver candlesticks. And silver candleholders. And the silver candelabra."

Charming nodded. "And have you anything in the way of"—he narrowed his eyes—"a silver bowl?"

The candlestick maker frowned. "No. If it's a candle or something to hold a candle in, you'll not find any better than these in my shop. If not, you won't see it here."

Charming flicked a glance at the list in my hand. "And of the candles," he said. "Do you make them in green? Perhaps a deep green?"

The candlestick maker gave a sad shake of his head. "Most folks around these parts aren't so adventurous. They like their candles plain." He brightened. "But if Your Highness would fancy a bit of color about the castle, I could dip you up a batch of whatever green you choose."

"We'll think on it," said Charming. "Thank you for your time, kind sir. I may return anon. The castle *is* in sore need of a candelabra."

21

A Butler in the Kitchens

We spent all this long day in the village."
Charming ran a brush down Darnell's flank one final
time. Darnell gave a soft nicker. "Are we any nearer to
unmasking the culprit?"

We were back at the castle. Charming had led
Darnell to his stall and pulled off saddle and bridle.
He'd given his steadfast steed a bucket of water and
a good brushing while I compared our lists and Ulff
plowed through the muffins in his basket.

We left Darnell in the stable, happily munching oats,
and crunched our way across the courtyard to the castle.

"If they're telling the truth"—I tapped the names on the list of suspects—"they're but innocent victims."

"And if not?" said Charming.

"Then between them," I said, "they have three spell ingredients, and the others—frog toe, water, lily pad, newt—would be easy enough to come by with but a visit to a pond. If the candlestick maker is lying as well, they have the silver bowl and candle."

Charming stopped. "You think they're all in on it together?"

I ran my gaze down the list. "I can't think any of them are in on it at all. Even if one of them had come by some previously unknown magic and managed to work out the ingredients for a frog potion and properly mix it, how would they have gotten it into the castle and near enough to Figgy so he'd drink it?"

"And make sure nobody else did," said Ulff.

I nodded. "I rather think someone stole the ingredients from them."

Charming gave a grim nod. "Stiltskin. It all comes back to him. I never knew he could cast spells, though."

I thought about this. "I can see him swiping the ingredients. But I can't see him mixing the potion. What motive has he for turning a prince to a frog? I think it more likely he snatched up the things when he saw a chance, then traded them to someone else."

"Someone who did have something to gain," said Ulff.

We'd reached the castle. We slipped in the side door, and Charming led the way to the kitchens.

"We'll suss out from Cook whether a silver bowl has gone missing," he whispered. "And whether the castle, perchance, harbors a green candle."

But when we reached the kitchens, we found Thistlewick slumped against Cook's big work table. Cook had her arm around him and patted his shoulder as she tried to get him to drink a cup of tea. A suitcase sat at Thistlewick's feet.

"Thistlewick!" Charming stopped short. "Whatever is the matter?"

Thistlewick bolted upright. "I apologize, Your Highness." He tugged his waistcoat to straighten it.

Charming stared at the suitcase. "What in the devil has happened?"

Thistlewick cleared his throat. "The queen, Ermintrude, insists that I've—I've—"

"She thinks he's taken that no-account son of hers," said Cook. "As if he ever would. But she squawked about it enough that now the king's relieved our Thistlewick of his duties."

Thistlewick dropped his head and stared at his flawlessly polished shoes.

Ulff and I looked at each other, eyes wide.

Charming gaped. "Relieved you of—but, no. Surely, you misheard."

"His majesty says it's merely a temporary measure," said Thistlewick. "Until we get this thing sorted. But for now I need to"—he set his mouth set in a firm, brave line—"leave."

Leave? I blinked. Thistlewick was a butler. As was *his* father and his father's father and his father before him. If he couldn't buttle, what would he do?

"You can't be cast out of your own castle." Ulff thrust a hand into his tunic and fished around till he pulled out a large brass key. "You can stay with me at the gatehouse. There's plenty of room."

He handed the key to Thistlewick.

"Thank you." Thistlewick slid the key into his waistcoat pocket. "It will be an honor to share quarters with a guard as fine as you."

"It shan't be for long." Charming clapped him on the shoulder. "We shall get this sorted. You have my word."

Thistlewick nodded. "I have every faith in you, Your Highness."

He picked up his bag and trudged from the kitchens, looking every inch like a prisoner marching to his cell.

"We must find who did this," said Charming. "Thistlewick can't stay out in that drafty gatehouse any longer than needs be. No offense, Ullf."

"None taken, Your Highness," said Ulff. "I like a stiff wind gusting through the living quarters myself, but most folks aren't partial to it."

We crept up four flights of winding stairs and down hallways and passageways. We had the list of spell ingredients and suspicions about who had swiped them from the village. But we still knew not who he'd swiped them *for*. Our hope was that Figgy could remember something, could give us some clue, however slight, of who it was could have done this to him.

We reached Angelica's bedchamber, and Charming gave a quiet rap on its thick oak door.

"It's us," he said.

The lock clicked open, and the three of us slipped inside.

Angelica looked up, eyes wide, face paler than it had

been since the day Sir Roderick had read the contract.

Charming placed an armored hand on her shoulder. "Whatever is wrong?"

Angelica let out a shuddering breath and turned her gaze toward the bed.

We turned to look.

Figgy was still on the pillow.

But instead of lounging smugly, licking chocolate from his toes, he lay listless, his skin sunken and dry and more yellow than green, his eyes glassed over. He took a breath, and his lungs sounded like a chair leg scraping across a stone floor.

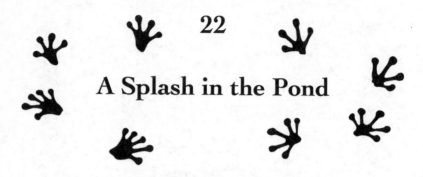

22

A Splash in the Pond

Stay with them." Charming placed a hand on my arm. "I shall return anon."

He turned and strode from the room. I locked the door shut behind him.

Wherever he went, he must have flown, for not many ticks of the clock passed by before a tap sounded at the bedchamber door and he slipped back inside. He bent over, hands on his knees, and gulped for breath.

The witch slipped into the bedchamber behind him.

I blinked.

Ulff's mouth dropped open.

"She can't reverse the spell." Charming's voice came out in a rasp. "But she'll do what she can to help."

The witch crossed to the bed, where Angelica was holding a cup of water to Figgy's thin, papery lips.

"Drink this, Figgy." Angelica jiggled the cup to rouse him. "Just take a sip."

The witch watched her.

"Frogs," she said, "drink through their skin."

Angelica blinked up at her. "Truly?"

The witch nodded. She spied the pile of empty chocolate wrappers on the bed.

She wrinkled her nose. "This is what you've been feeding him?"

"It's what he wanted," said Angelica.

"It's not what frogs eat." The witch eyed the dishpan, upturned and discarded on the rug. "We need to get him to the garden pond. He needs mud and pond water and flies."

We loaded Figgy into the dishpan. He was heavier than I expected for a frog. But he *was* enormous.

Between us, Ulff and I lugged him from Angelica's bedchamber. Charming strode a pace ahead of us, half hiding us from view. The witch and Angelica brought up the rear, darting glances behind us as we wove our way through hallways and passages, down four flights of winding stairs, and out the side door by the kitchens.

We crunched across the courtyard to the garden.

Charming lifted Figgy from the dishpan and set him on a lily pad.

Figgy drooped to his side and sighed.

Angelica darted about the garden until she trapped a fly. She brought it back to the pond and held it to his lips.

"Come on, Figbert," she told him. "It's good for you. Probably."

Figbert lolled out his tongue, and Angelica placed the fly on it. He grimaced, but swallowed.

"Huh," he croaked. "Not as bad as I . . . *ribbit*."

Angelica tipped her head. "That's new." She frowned. "He's never ribbited before."

Angelica and the witch splashed Figbert with pond water. Charming, Ulff, and I dashed about, trapping more flies. We brought them back to Angelica.

As she fed them to him, I studied the frog. Figgy's skin seemed to have greened up a bit, and his breath sounded more normal, more like actual breathing than the grinding of walnut shells.

Angelica held out a fly to him. "Try another. I think they're helping, Figbert."

"Figbert?" A voice pierced the air.

We looked up.

Queen Ermintrude barreled into the garden, her maid on her heels. Sir Roderick followed, lifting his steps high as he picked his way through the vines and flowers.

Ermintrude knelt at the edge of the pond. She peered into Figbert's eyes.

"Figgy?" she cried. "Is that you?"

Figgy gave her a froggy smile. "Hello—*croooaaak*—Mother."

185

23

A Princess and a Frog

Queen Ermintrude bundled Figbert into her robes and between the two of them, she and Lucy lugged Figgy into the castle. Charming, Ulff, Angelica, and I followed. Sir Roderick rather skulked along behind. I glanced about for the witch, but she had vanished.

"Who could blame her?" muttered Ulff. "With the queen throwing blame far and wide, it wouldn't be long afore some of it landed on that lovely lass."

"And with her being a witch," I said, "blame would most likely stick."

We followed Charming and Angelica up the stairs and into the king's library.

We arrived in time to see the queen slide Figbert onto the king's desk. Water from the garden pond slopped onto the king's papers.

"This," Ermintrude bellowed at the king, "is what your ill-mannered, ill-tempered, ill-behaved princess has done to my Froggy—I mean Figgy."

The king pulled his head back and stared. Lucy pulled a cloth from her skirt and tried to press it to her mistress's forehead. Her mistress batted it away. Sir Roderick leaned casually against the fireplace and pulled the contract scroll from his robes.

"This"—the king blinked—"is Prince Figbert?"

Ermintrude sniffed. "Yes."

"I certainly—*ribbit*," said Figgy.

The king pulled back.

Charming stepped forward. "The good news is we found him," he said.

"The bad news is he's a frog," said Ulff.

"The worse news"—Angelica swallowed—"is we don't know how to turn him back."

Ermintrude turned on her. Her eyes blazed. "Oh, I know how you will turn him back."

"No!" I stepped in front of Angelica, then blinked in confusion at my sudden show of gallantry. I knew not where it came from.

Charming stepped in front of the both of us. "The princess has no magical power. She did not cast this spell."

"Really." Ermintrude raised an eyebrow. "Then who did, pray tell?"

"We . . . well . . ." Charming swallowed. "we're still—"

"They don't—*crooooaaak*—know," said Figgy.

"Yet," said Charming. "We don't know yet."

Figbert's croak had gotten raspier, pierced through with *ribbit*s and *croak*s. He flicked his tongue to catch a fly. Then he spied a large flowerpot on the windowsill. He hopped over, climbed into it, and burrowed down in the moist dirt.

"Figgy!" cried his mother.

But Figgy was too distracted by a gnat for even a quick *ribbit*.

Ermintrude sank onto the window seat and gazed at him. Lucy bustled about her, fluttering her with a fan.

"It's bad enough he's a frog," the queen moaned. "But I think he's getting froggier."

I thought about this. When frog Figbert used princely things like pillows and ate princely food like chocolate, he acted much like a prince. He talked like a prince. He ordered everyone around like a price.

But all that lounging on a pillow eating truffles made him sick. Frog things—the pond, flies, mud—seemed to cure him. I glanced at him now, puffing his throat out and in with his croaks. But frog things seemed to make him act like a frog.

Croooaaaak.

The sound floated through the library, softer and a bit, well, sweeter, than Figgy's usual gravelly barks.

I glanced at the flowerpot. Figbert sat very still, his froggy head cocked to one side.

Croooaaaak.

There it was again. Only Figgy hadn't croaked it.

He hopped from the pot to the window.

Croooaaaak.

The sound came again. It was another frog. Outside. In the garden.

Figgy placed a webbed foot against the glass and gazed longingly at the garden pond below. Then he

190

looked back at his mother and placed another webbed foot against her hand. He seemed to be torn between his new nature and his old. And he could only choose one.

He gave a low mournful croak. Frog tears welled in his eyes.

Tears welled in Angelica's, too. For I was not the only one watching.

"I can't take him from his mother," Angelica whispered.

She leaned toward Figbert. She squeezed shut her eyes. She puckered her lips. A tear ran down her cheek.

"Angelica, no!" roared the king.

But Angelica leaned closer.

Then closer still.

Until her lips touched Figgy's head.

She gave him a kiss.

In that instant, the candles flared. The parchment scroll in Roderick's hand began to glow. It quivered, and a soft *plink* echoed through the room.

A smile slid across Roderick's face.

"The deal," he said, "is sealed."

The king groaned.

Charming moaned.

Ulff and I gasped.

Someone croaked. "What about—*ribbit*—me?"

We all turned.

Figbert was perched on the windowsill.

"I'm still a—*crooooooak*." He flicked his tongue at the gnat.

"Oh, no." Angelica's face grew pale. "It didn't work. I'm betrothed . . . to a frog."

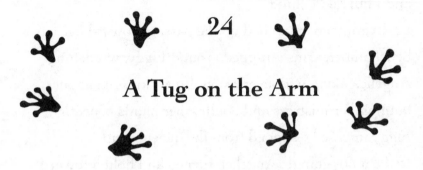

24

A Tug on the Arm

𝕴 will not stay one moment more in this miserable kingdom!"

"*Croooaaak,*" said Figgy.

Queen Ermintrude heaved Figgy from the king's table, bundled him into her robes, and lugged him from the library. Lucy gathered up handkerchief and fan and scuttered after her.

"Oww!" cried Angelica. She rubbed her upper arm. "Something's—"

She stumbled from the library, her upper arm held out as if something were chained to it and pulling her along.

Charming bounded after her. The king followed. Ulff and I hurried behind.

Ermintrude marched up the passage toward her bedchamber, arms wrapped around Figgy, wrenching Angelica along with every step. Lucy skittered about, fanning her mistress and holding her hands beneath Figgy in case he slipped from the queen's grip.

"I'm not going!" Angelica turned and bolted toward her father.

She took two steps and lurched to a stop, as if she'd reached the end of a chain.

"Aaah!" She rubbed her upper arms and planted her feet, but the unseen chain dragged her back.

I looked at Ulff. He looked at me, eyes wide, bristly face drained of its redness. And most of its bristliness.

"Looks like that Roderick *was* right about something in his egg-rotted life." Ulff gulped. "The contract's binding. It's binding up her very arms."

"You're betrothed to Prince Figbert," Queen Ermintrude told Angelica through gritted teeth. "You'll never get away from him, whether or not I find a way to unfrog him."

Ermintrude shifted Figgy in her arms, and Angelica was jerked farther away.

"Please." The king spread his arms. "You and Prince Figbert are welcome to live in the castle as long as you like. You can have your own apartments. Figbert can have his own . . . pond. You can have anything you like. Stay so Angelica can be in her home. With me."

Queen Ermintrude arched an eyebrow. "We have a contract." Her voice was sharp and hard. "I will be taking my son, your wretch of a daughter, my payment—"

"And your maid," said Lucy.

"—and leaving," said Ermintrude.

The king let out a heavy sigh. He seemed to slump within his robes.

"Very well," he said. "I'll have my servants pack your bags."

"No!" Ermintrude gasped. She cleared her throat and took a breath. "I mean, how very thoughtful of you, but my maid can easily pack our things herself. I don't want to be an imposition."

I frowned. That was odd.

"She never minded being an imposition before," said Ulff.

The queen turned and marched down the corridor, Figgy in her arms, Angelica lurching behind.

"We shall leave," she said, "within the hour."

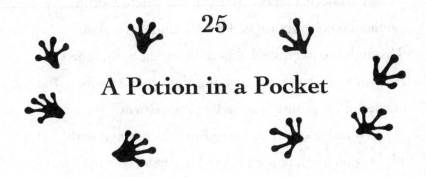

25

A Potion in a Pocket

Queen Ermintrude swept toward the carriage, cradling Figgy in her arms. A cloud of sweet, flowery perfume swirled in her wake.

Lucy heaved their bags and cases into the carriage with *thump*s and *bang*s and, in the case of one large trunk, a muffled *clank*.

Angelica broke into a sob, threw her arms around her father's waist, and clung to him.

The king wrapped his arms around her and clung back. Cook and the castle servants—save Thistlewick—clustered outside the doorway, swallowing back tears.

They were not the only ones watching.

Sir Roderick stood apart, in the shadow of the castle, the contract tucked firmly under his arm. Through the narrowed slits of his eyes, he watched Angelica and the king clasping tight to each other. The corner of his mouth quirked in amusement.

Ermintrude settled herself in the carriage with Figbert on her lap, then leaned her head toward the open carriage door.

"Let's get on with it, *princess*." Her voice cut like a dagger through the courtyard. "I've wasted enough time at this castle."

Angelica wiped her eyes, blew her nose, and gave her father one last squeeze. She turned, took a shuddering breath, and climbed into the carriage.

Lucy whisked past us to climb in after her.

A cloud of scent swirled about Lucy, too. But not the sweet, flowery scent of her mistress. I sniffed. This was savory. And herbal. And a little rank. More befitting of maid than mistress, perhaps.

But as her skirts brushed the carriage door, something rattled, then clinked.

I frowned. Why would a maid rattle and clink? She carried with her a fan at all times, and a soft cloth to comfort the queen. But neither fan nor cloth would rattle and clink. And what was it that gave her that distinctive scent? Tea for her mistress, perhaps. A few herbs.

My mouth dropped open.

I thought of Lucy's devotion to her mistress. I thought of the teas and tonics she concocted for her. I thought of her bumping into Stiltskin in the village and of him speaking to her. I thought of Stiltskin's penchant for pilfering and how we'd suspected it was he who stole the spices from the butcher and the baker, most likely to trade them to someone else.

I thought of how Figgy had insisted Lucy bring him cocoa. And of her dogged search to find him after he'd disappeared—around the garden pond and moat. I glanced at the carriage, at the fat green leaf painted on its top, and I thought of the queen's scroll, stamped with the queen's imprint on a wax seal of the deepest green.

I thought how Lucy would never do anything to hurt her mistress. How all she ever wanted was to help her.

I thought all these thoughts, and I opened my mouth.

"STOP!" I cried.

Everyone turned.

"Nobbin." Charming frowned. "Is something wrong?"

"Yes." I kept my voice low. "Or maybe no. Maybe something is about to turn very right." I tipped my head toward Lucy. "Do you recognize the scent of her?"

Charming sniffed. "Is it . . . soup? Chicken noodle. Or no—mushroom."

Cook shook her head. She stepped forward. She gave a sniff.

"It's mugwort," she said. "And a bit of cinnamon. And sugar, too, methinks." She sniffed again and wrinkled her nose. "And another smell, not as pleasant. Could it be"—she wrinkled her nose—"eye of newt? Oh! And a musty bit of frog toe."

Charming stared at her. "You know the scent of frog toe?"

Cook shrugged.

"I believe," I said, "the queen's maid carries a bottle of it in her pocket."

"No." Lucy shook her head back and forth. "I don't. I don't even know what that is."

"Yes," said Charming. "I believe you do."

The king wiped his eyes and blew his nose.

"I'd like to see what's in your pockets," he told Lucy.

Lucy swallowed. She darted her panicked gaze toward the king, then at the carriage. She took a quick step toward it, thinking to make her escape. A large footman moved to block her path, and she stopped, no doubt to think again.

She turned to the king, gave another long swallow, and reached into her pockets.

From one pocket, she pulled bottles of herbs. From another, jars of liquid. She reached into her skirts and drew out a spoon, a silver bowl, an assortment of feathers and stones, a green candle, and a small wand. She set it all down in a small pile at her feet.

Charming stared at it in wonder. "Great flipping flapjacks."

The king shook his head. "And to think she hid it all in her skirts."

"What is taking so long?" Ermintrude thrust her head from the carriage window. She saw Lucy standing, pockets outturned, bottles and jars at her feet. "What on—is that the candle I use for my wax seal? And my silver bowl?"

Charming tipped his head toward Lucy. "It was she, Your Majesty, who turned young Figbert into a frog."

Lucy's lips quivered. She turned tear-filled eyes toward her mistress.

"I—it was an accident!" she cried. "Or at least, a surprise. I didn't think it would work. I've been trying my hand at magic, attempting spells to reverse Your Majesty's bad fortune, or at least relieve your headaches, but nothing worked. I was a magical failure."

The king raised an eyebrow.

"But suddenly, it didn't matter." Lucy's face brightened. "Not once we got word to come fetch the princess. That was a reversal of fortune right there, that was." She glanced at the king.

He nodded. "Continue."

Lucy took a breath. "But then the princess refused to come. She said she'd rather kiss a frog, and that gave me an idea. If our prince were a frog, maybe she *would* kiss him, since that's what princesses are supposed to do. So I mixed a frog potion and stirred it into his cocoa, and what do you know? It worked!" She leaned toward her mistress. "No one was more surprised than me, I can tell you that."

"You—you—" Ermintrude sputtered. "*You* turned my Figgy into this—this—reptile?"

"Amphibian," said Lucy. "Prince Figbert is an amphibian."

"But not for long, madame."

Charming stepped forward. He pulled himself up to his full princely height and placed a gallant, armored hand on Lucy's arm.

"You were very clever," he told her. "But now that the spell has done its part, you must unfrog him."

"I—" Lucy stared at her shoes. "I'm not sure I can. My spells never work, so I've never thought how to reverse them. I believed the kiss would surely work." She let out a breath. "But it didn't."

"The witch said that whoever cast the spell should do what they did before," I whispered to Charming. "Only backward."

"Quite right." Charming turned to the maid. "Perhaps you need only carry out the spell exactly as you did at first, but this time in reverse."

Lucy looked up at him. "I can try," she said.

"*Ribbit,*" said Figgy.

26

A Flicker of the Flame

Lucy spread her bottles and jars, bowl and spoons, candle, feathers, stones, and wand across the top of the king's wide desk.

She stared at her pile of ingredients.

"You can do this," said Charming.

Lucy gulped. "I need to remember how I did it the first time, so I can turn it around and do it backward."

She closed her eyes and began moving her lips.

We were back in the king's library. The king had swept the books and scrolls from his desk, and Queen Ermintrude had hoisted Figgy onto the desktop. The queen stood beside him, squeezing the edge of the desk in a white-knuckled grip.

The king and Prince Charming stood side by side in front of the fire, Angelica before them, her fingers, arms, and legs crossed for luck. The king placed his hands protectively on her shoulders. Ulff and I scuttled off to the side.

As we leaned forward, intent on Lucy's every move, the tension in the room nearly squeezed the air from my lungs. Only Sir Roderick seemed untouched by it.

Ulff tipped his head toward the window seat, where Sir Roderick lounged, legs crossed, the edge of the contract peeking out from his robes.

I nodded. "He cares not whether Figgy is prince or frog. He cares only that his deal is sealed."

Lucy's lips stopped moving. She frowned and opened her eyes.

She plunged a hand in her pocket, pulled out a small scrap of paper, and held it in her palm as she studied it. She gave a nod and thrust the slip back into her pocket.

She lit the candle and pulled the bowl to the center of the table, then arranged feathers and stones in a circle around it.

Ulff frowned. "The witch didn't mention feathers

and stones," he whispered.

"I think she's just being overvigilant," I said.

Lucy pulled the stoppers from the bottles and jars.

"Oof!" Ulff waved a hand in front of his nose.

The king and Charming turned their heads away. The queen clapped a hand over her mouth. Angelica near well gagged.

I coughed and blinked, my eyes burning from the stench that roiled from the maid's bottles.

"Sorry." Lucy scrunched her face into an apology. "It is rank, I know. But it'll soon fade." She frowned. "Or maybe the stink of it burns your nose enough you stop smelling altogether." She brightened. "Either way, you soon won't notice the odor."

She thrust a hand in her pocket, gave another quick peek at a scrap of paper, then began measuring and pouring, mixing and stirring.

At last, she set her spoon on the table and snatched up her wand. She held the silver bowl over the flame of the green candle. She blinked.

She set the bowl down and pulled the paper scrap from her pocket once more. She smoothed it on the table and studied it, her lips moving over the words.

She gave a nod, picked up her wand once more, and

209

spoke. "True and fond kiss a by snapped be only can."

Ulff leaned toward me. "What's she saying?"

"The spell," I said. "She's reciting it backward."

"Brew this by bestowed," she continued, "charming frogified the."

She peered into the bowl.

Ulff and I leaned in for a better look, as did the queen, the king, Charming, and Angelica.

A cloud of steam—greenish and pungent—rose from the bowl. Inside, a thick mixture bubbled.

Lucy gave it one last swirl, set the bowl on the table, and rubbed her hands down her gown.

She looked up. "It's ready," she said. "I hope."

Lucy dipped the spoon into the mixing bowl to scoop up some of the potion. She held it out to Figgy.

He flicked his tongue and bumped it. The spoon tipped, spilling half the potion down Lucy's gown. She tried again. Figgy turned his head away.

Lucy's face crumpled. "He doesn't like it."

"What if we can't get him to drink it?" The queen's voice trembled.

Angelica knotted her face in thought. She stepped to the desk and took the spoon from Lucy's hand.

"Frogs," she said, "drink through their skin."

Angelica dripped the potion onto Figgy's belly
and rubbed it in with the spoon. In that instant, a gust
swirled through the room. The draperies billowed, and
the candle flickered.

Figgy croaked.

He made a soft *ribbit*.

He groused.

He grumbled.

He let out a belch.

And then the green began fading from his skin.

"Oh!" cried the queen.

"It's working," whispered Lucy, her voice filled with
surprise.

Figgy's head grew larger. And rounder—although
not *that* round, since his true prince head was rather flat
in the first place. His ears popped out, then his nose.
His shoulders grew wider so that his neck emerged.
And then—

—he stopped.

We watched. We held our breaths.

But nothing happened.

Figbert sat in the middle of the king's great desk, with
head and shoulders of a prince, but body still of a frog.

Lucy shook her head wildly and backed away.

Angelica spooned more potion over Figgy and rubbed it in. She even managed to pour a bit down his throat.

He sputtered and gagged.

But he stayed half frog.

"The witch *said* a reverse potion could make it worse," Ulff muttered.

I nodded. "This is definitely worse."

"You!" The queen turned on Lucy, flames fairly bursting from her eyes. "You turned my Figgy into this—this—creature. You mixed up this brew—"

Brew? I blinked. Lucy had recited something about the brew. I tried to recall it: *Brew this by bestowed.* I switched the words around.

"Bestowed by this brew," I murmured.

Ulff gave me a puzzled look. The queen still raged at her maid.

What else had Lucy said? I closed my eyes and concentrated. *True and fond kiss a by snapped be only can.*

I popped my eyes open. "Can only be snapped by a kiss fond and true!"

The queen stopped. Lucy gasped. Figgy let out a long *riiibbbiiiit.* Everyone turned to look at me.

"Can only be snapped by a kiss fond and true," I said

again. "That's why Angelica's kiss didn't work. Her kiss wasn't true."

"And it sure wasn't fond," said Ulff.

I turned to Lucy. "Kiss him," I said.

"What?" She gave me a horrified look.

"Kiss him," I told her. "You're fond of the prince."

"Well, yes," she said, "but—"

"And you're true," I said. "I've never known a maid more true to a mistress and her family."

"But—I'm not a princess," she said.

"Your spell doesn't require one," I said.

Lucy furrowed her brow in thought. Her lips moved as she mouthed the words of her spell. "A kiss fond and true," she murmured. She looked up. "I *meant* it to be a kiss from a princess—"

"But you didn't *say* it," said Ulff.

She blinked. "I didn't."

She eyed Figgy. She swallowed. She gripped the edge of the table and leaned sideways toward the prince. Frog. Prince. She puckered her lips and shot a look at me.

I gave her an encouraging nod.

Lucy leaned closer, then closer still, until her lips

213

touched the top of Figbert's head. She gave him a kiss and jumped back.

The flame flickered, and the drapes billowed once more.

"*Crooooaaaak*," croaked Figgy.

His legs began to grow. Longer, then longer still. The legs in the front reshaped into arms. He grew, taller and taller, but still not *that* tall, and the webs of his feet turned into toes.

Finally, perched on the king's desk, sat Prince Figbert. The drapes settled, and the flicker of the flame grew still.

"Figgy!" The queen drew Prince Figbert in her arms. "You're back."

Figgy looked down at himself. "I'm—*currroooak*—a prince," he said.

Angelica swallowed.

"And I'm still betrothed to him," she whispered.

27

A Clank in the Trunk

With a click of the door latch and a *"Ho!"* from the driver, the gleaming black carriage with the fat green leaf trundled from the castle.

Queen Ermintrude was on board. And Prince Figbert. He was fully a prince now, but his tongue still darted out when a fly buzzed past.

Lucy was with them. The queen had first thought to cast her out, then thought again. Lucy *had* managed to cast a successful spell, even if that spell frogged Figgy. And she had also managed to reverse it, which showed great magical promise.

The queen weighed these thoughts and announced that she would take Lucy home with her.

"A bit of magic, even if unreliable, may come in handy," she said.

Angelica, too, was on board. She pressed her face to the window as the carriage rolled away.

Thistlewick had slipped from the gatehouse to bid her farewell. He stood like a soldier beside the open gate, ready to wave goodbye. As he waited, he lifted a gloved hand to catch a tear before it spilled down his cheek.

I stood with Ulff, Charming, and the king before the castle, staring after Angelica. I was glad Lucy was with her. She might, in time, look after Angelica as she looked after the queen. I thought of all the things Lucy did for her mistress. Mending her hems. Fanning her endlessly. Giving her herbal tea and cold compresses. Using every ounce of her strength to load bags and trunks onto the carriage, no matter how heavy or—

I blinked.

—or noisy.

"The clank!" I said.

I glanced at Sir Roderick, who stood by the castle door, arms crossed, the contract tight in his grasp.

When he gazed back, his eyes were two hard, black cinders burning a hole through my very chest.

I turned and leaned toward Charming.

"I was worried about the clink," I whispered, "but I forgot the clank. I know where the silver tea set is."

Charming turned to me. "And the candelabra?"

I nodded. "They're in Queen Ermintrude's trunk, the last one Lucy heaved onto the carriage."

"Then we must stop them." Charming took a step toward the carriage.

We had kept our voices low, but Sir Roderick must have seen us glancing at him. And at the contract. And the carriage.

He, too, took a step toward the carriage. Then another. And another. And before I knew it, he had passed us.

"Go!" Roderick cried out to the carriage driver. "Spur the horses. Make haste. Leave this castle at once!"

The carriage driver shot a confused frown over his shoulder, then lifted the reins and gave them a brisk shake to spur the horses.

But in that moment, Thistlewick stepped in front of the gate. He held up one hand.

"Stop!" he ordered.

"Ho!" The carriage driver pulled back on the reins.

But the horses had already picked up speed.

They thundered toward Thistlewick, boring down upon him.

The castle butler stood his ground. He held his hand in the air, unwavering.

The driver, still yanking hard, finally reined in his team. They came to a stop mere inches from Thistlewick, their steamy hot breath snorting over his face.

28

A Glint of the Sun

We marched to the carriage—Charming, the king, Ulff, and me, followed by a pair of footmen. The king gave a nod. The footmen lifted Queen Ermintrude's large trunk from the carriage and set it on the cobblestone drive.

Queen Ermintrude jutted her head from the carriage window.

"What is the meaning of this?" she cried.

"Good sirs," Charming told the footmen, "open that trunk."

"Don't you dare!" shrieked Ermintrude. "That trunk is private proper—"

One of the footmen unlatched the trunk, and the other swung open the lid.

"That is *mine*!" The queen's shriek turned to screech.

She rattled the door handle, trying to get out, but the king flipped the bolt on the outside.

"How dare you!" cried the queen.

The king strode to the trunk. We all gathered round and peered inside. There, bundled between the queen's skirts, were the good silver tea set and the king's candelabra.

And a silver mirror.

And a jeweled brooch.

And a gilt picture frame, a bust of the king from the library, and a pair of fur-lined slippers.

And Thistlewick's gold-handled magnifying glass.

"My glass!" Thistlewick lifted it from the trunk and held it to his heart.

Ulff blinked. "That queen was busier than we thought."

The king raised his head and glared at the queen.

"What," he said, "are these things doing in your trunk?"

The queen lifted her nose in the air. "I've never seen those things before in my life," she said. "They must have . . . fallen into my trunk somehow, or were perhaps put there by—by—my maid. Yes! My maid. We've all seen how unreliable she is."

"Your *Majesty*!" Lucy's hurt voice echoed from inside the carriage.

The king shook his head and turned back to the trunk.

"I *am* truly puzzled," he said. "Why would you take these things?"

"I didn't!" said the queen. She rattled the door handle once more. "It was that butler of yours."

"I beg your pardon?" said Thistlewick.

"He put them there," said the queen. "To spite me."

"He could hardly do that from the gatehouse." The king sighed and looked to Charming.

Charming raised an armored finger in the air, then flicked a glance at me.

"The queen is not as wealthy as she seems," I whispered.

"Despite her lavish gowns and the opulent palace she claims to live in," said Charming, "Queen Ermintrude's fortunes have indeed reversed, just as the maid Lucy has said."

"That's why she wanted Angelica," I whispered.

"Which is why she agreed to take Angelica under her wing," said Charming.

"I was doing you a favor," said the queen.

"Because with Angelica," Charming continued, "came a great deal of wealth, which the queen sorely needed."

"Yes, yes." The king waved a hand. "But the deal was sealed, and she was getting the wealth. Why did she need"—he motioned toward the trunk—"all this?"

"She wanted to be sure," I whispered.

"She wasn't certain you would go through with the agreement in the end," said Charming.

"That's right!" said the queen. "I knew you were unreliable from the start."

"She needed insurance," Charming went on, "in case you had a change of heart."

"Which you did," said the queen.

"She began snatching up silver and baubles and jewels, hiding them in her skirts, I would imagine." At this last bit, Charming looked at me.

I nodded.

"Yes, in her skirts," he said. "Then stashed them in her trunk to take back with her."

"What choice did you give me?" screeched the queen.

As her voice echoed across the courtyard, she realized what she'd just said.

"I mean, of course I didn't . . . take anything." She snapped shut her mouth and pulled her head back into the carriage.

"And now," said Charming, "we shall return the baubles to their rightful place in the castle."

One by one, he began pulling the silver and jewels from the trunk—as well as the rather large bag of coins the king had given Queen Ermintrude as payment. As Charming lifted the picture frame, a ray of sunlight caught on one of its gilt corners. The light reflected off the frame, near blinding us, and lit on the scroll under Roderick's arm.

Sir Roderick glanced down at it with a start.

The scroll began glowing, and a soft *plink* echoed over the roadway.

"Oh!" A small yelp echoed from the carriage.

The carriage door opened, and Angelica tumbled out.

She stood, eyes wide, mouth open. She rubbed her upper arms, then gazed down at them.

She flexed her arms and spread them wide.

She looked up. "The bond, I think, is broken."

The contract began smoldering. Roderick plucked it from under his arm and tossed it to the ground just as it burst into flames.

Ulff and I watched it burn.

"Huh," he said. "Looks like a breach."

I nodded. "The queen was stealing, or, as Sir Roderick explained it, deceiving the king into providing something above and beyond the terms listed in the contract."

I watched Sir Roderick trying to stomp out the flames.

"Rendering it null."

Stomp.

"And."

Stomp. Stomp.

"Void."

Stomp. Stomp, stomp.

The last of the parchment sizzled and disappeared in a puff of smoke.

29

A Stroke of Luck

Queen Ermintrude peered from the carriage window. Her lips quivered. She clutched a hand to her chest.

Lucy had climbed out to repack the queen's skirts into the trunk. She held a lace fan to the carriage window and fluttered it over her mistress's face.

One of the footmen waved a thumb toward the queen. "Should we take her to the dungeon, Your Majesty?"

"Oh!" The queen gave a strangled cry.

The king shook his head. "She's spent enough time in my castle. I'll not have her sully it longer."

The queen sank back in her seat.

Lucy heaved the trunk onto the carriage and turned to climb inside.

"You sure you want to go back?" Ulff tipped his head toward the carriage. "With her?"

"Oh, yes." Lucy gave a contented sigh. "I'm ever so grateful to be her lady's maid."

Ulff frowned. "Truly?"

Lucy nodded. "I wasn't more than a scullery maid before and had no hope of ever being anything more. Not until the queen lost her riches. She had to keep letting servants go, one by one, till in the end there was only me. She couldn't afford a true lady's maid. Her choice was either me or nothing. I'm ever so grateful she didn't choose nothing."

She reached for the carriage handle, then stopped.

"I never thought of it before, but I never would've had this good fortune if the queen hadn't had bad." She shook her head. "You can be sure I'll be looking out for bad fortune in the future. You never know what bright thing might come of it."

She climbed into the carriage. And with the click of the door latch and a *"Ho!"* from the driver, the gleaming black carriage with the fat green leaf trundled from the castle.

For good, this time.

"Mother!" Figbert's voice drifted back to us. "Does this mean I'm *not* getting a real steed?"

After they'd gone and we were walking back to the castle, Angelica looked up at her father.

"I'll do better," she said. "I'll stop climbing down the tower, and I'll tell the dwarfs to find another fielder. I'll practice waving and curtsying and eating and sitting and not tripping over my gown. And I won't shoot bits of dessert across the table at houseguests. Or think horrible thoughts about them. Or call them names when they aren't listening."

"Call them names?" The king raised an eyebrow. "You did that?"

Angelica nodded.

The king smiled. "Me, too."

Angelica took a breath. "I'll be a proper princess," she told him. "I promise."

The king put his arm around her shoulders.

"Angelica," he said. "You cast aside your own happiness, your future, your very life, in truth, to save someone else—a prince who, if we're honest, little deserved your kindness. You're more of a princess than all the princesses in all the fairy tales joined together. You're more of a princess than ever I could have wished for." He looked down at her. "Besides, who wants to practice waving and curtsying and eating and sitting when there are rounders games to be played?"

30

A Princess with a Treasure

ou there." The king waved a finger toward me.
"Nobbin."

We were on the castle balcony once again. The
sun's first rays cast a soft glow over the castle walls.
The grass sparkled with dew in the courtyard below.
Thistlewick kept a sharp eye on the pair of footmen who
made their way through the crowd, serving tea.

The king frowned. "Does the princess seem
nervous?"

I peered across the courtyard. At the far end,

Princess Angelica held the reins of her new filly, a fearless and lanky horse she'd named Rounders.

Sunlight shone brightly over princess and horse. Angelica's curls glistened. Her face glowed. A brilliant smile stretched across her face.

"No, sire," I said.

"She looks calm," I said.

"Unruffled," I said.

The princess pressed her cheek to Rounders's neck and gave the horse a nuzzle.

"Happy to be doing what she's doing," said I.

The king nodded and sat back in his throne. "That's what I was hoping for," he said.

At the other end of the courtyard, the tower soared to the sky, dark against the morning's soft light. Prince Charming clanked back and forth at its base, paging through notes, checking items off a list, tugging at the rope that dangled from the tower window to check the fastness of it. At last, he unfurled a small flag emblazoned with the king's colors.

Charming raised the flag.

And according to the lesson plan, this is what was supposed to happen next:

1. At Charming's signal, Angelica would leap onto Rounders's back.

2. Angelica and Rounders would gallop across the courtyard to the tower, where the treasure (not damsel, though the dwarfs were so happy to have Angelica back on the team, they had volunteered to step in as substitute damsels should it become necessary) was being held.

3. Angelica would neatly dismount, climb the rope

(in this case, actual rope, not rope meant to be hair, which is useless for climbing, as Angelica pointed out, repeatedly), and hoist herself through the tower window.

4. She would climb back down, carrying the treasure and passing the test of a True Princess.

This is what actually happened:

With a whip of his wrist, Charming lowered the flag. Angelica leapt for Rounders's saddle, neatly sliding one foot into the stirrup and swinging her other leg over the horse.

She spurred Rounders on, and horse and rider galloped across the courtyard. Angelica's hair whipped around her in a whirlwind of curls. Rounders's mane and tail flew out behind as her hooves pounded the grass.

When they reached the tower, Angelica took hold of the rope and began climbing. She reached the top and slipped through the tower window.

A moment later, she leaned back out.

"I have it!" She flung an arm in the air. Clutched in her hand were one lucky mitten and one woolen sock.

"She did it!" cried the dwarfs.

"Huzzah!" cheered the crowd.

Angelica swung her leg out the window and climbed down.

When she reached the courtyard, she handed the mitten to Charming. He tucked it into his gauntlet.

She took up Rounders's reins, gave the filly a scratch, and tucked the lucky sock into her sleeve.

"That's our princess," said Thistlewick.

"She is indeed," said the king.

Author's Note
Frogs and Games

Croaked! includes a lot of frog magic, so you may have thought *all* the frog parts were made up. But, no. Except for that business about a character turning into a frog, everything I wrote about frogs is true.

Frogs really do drink through their skin. They also breathe that way. Most frogs have lungs, but they absorb a lot of their oxygen directly through their skin. To take in the oxygen, their skin must stay moist. If their skin dries out, it can't absorb oxygen or get rid of carbon dioxide. That's why the frog in *Croaked!* had to get to the pond—its skin was too dry to breathe!

Frogs also shed their skin. This comes in handy when you need to gather toe of frog for a frog spell—you don't need to hurt a poor frog to get it. You can just wait till it sheds and use a bit of the toe skin in your potion. You'll need to be quick, though. Frog skin is full of protein and is very nutritious for frogs. So as soon as a frog sheds its skin, it eats it.

Here's a frog fact that won't help with a spell but is fun to know: Frogs swallow with their eyes. When frogs eat, their eyeballs sink down into their mouths and push the food backward down their throats.

Just as the frog parts are true, so are the games Princess Angelica likes to play. Her favorite sport is rounders, which is similar to baseball or softball. People began playing rounders in England several hundred years ago, and kids still play rounders in England and Ireland today.

In baseball, the player who throws the ball toward the batter is called the pitcher. In rounders, this player is called the bowler, and the bowler tosses the ball underhand. Each batter gets only one good ball, and they have to run whether they hit it—or even swing at it—or not. Rounders bats are shorter than baseball bats, and batters usually hold and swing the bat with one hand. The batter runs around bases, similar to baseball, but the bases aren't low, square canvas bags. They are sticks poked into the ground.

When Angelica gets bored at castle parties, she likes to play piquet (pronounced pee-KAY). Piquet originated in France more than 400 years ago. It is a card game for two players—which is why Angelica has to talk one of the footmen into playing it with her. After dealing and sorting the cards, each player lays down one card in each trick, or round of play. The object of the game is to have the best card in each trick and collect the most points.

The footmen have never said so, but I suspect they let Angelica win.